Aimee is a mother of one. When she is not looking after her son, she is in her office, writing fiction. She resides in Northern Alberta, where she was born and raised.

Thank you to everyone who has helped me while writing the Basilisks Series. It took an army behind me to bring *The Basilisks* and *The Runaway Basilisk* to life.

Thank you, Paige, for giving me feedback on *The Basilisks*, which gave me the idea to bring Haley and Archie to life.

Thank you, Delaney, for talking me down when I got scared and anxious. If it wasn't for you, I would have never made this huge leap.

Thank you, Batuhan, for helping me with the ins and outs of getting inside a male's head.

Thank you, Rylan, for being my rock, and being the kind of friend, I was able to base a friendship off of.

To everyone who had to repeat things to me multiple times while writing the *Basilisk* books, knowing that I was stuck in the world of my fictional Mafia, I love you all and thank you to everyone who stood behind me encouraging me to be the very best.

None of this would be possible if it wasn't for the people who love me.

Aimee Danroth

THE RUNAWAY BASILISK

Chapter 1

Hayley

"No one's going to know." I place my cigarette in my teeth fumbling for the lighter somewhere in my purse.

"Yes, Hayley, no one will fucking know." My brother's sarcasm is undeniable. "You just signed your death sentence."

"Joshua, stop being so damn dramatic." I glance around the courtyard, I need to be careful with what I say, there are a lot of people around that it could take only a few words that leave my lips and it would leave them with an entirely different story.

He sighs. "Do you have a friend yet at least?"

I pull the phone away from my ear covering the mouthpiece looking at a random girl with short auburn beside me. "Do me a solid and say hi, will you?"

She scans my skinny jeans, my knee-high boots and a sweater that is almost two sizes too big for me. She rolls her eyes, "Hi mate." Her attention is brought back to the group of people.

I put my phone to my ear, Josh's laughter erupts in the phone. Hearing his laugh is sending a dull ache through my chest, it has only been a few days since I saw him in New York. I am homesick, already.

I flick my cigarette, closing my eyes trying to remind myself why I left. "I'll be okay. I just need you and Spencer to try and soften the blow."

"You know we will. I am calling you every week. Good night."

I hang up the phone, squeezing it in my palm. There have been eight of us since we were born. I'm only blood related to two of them. We cling onto each other and my leaving was the single hardest thing I've ever had to do, and that says a lot. As hard as it is to be away from them, it is also the easiest thing I've ever had to do. Studying abroad is either my death sentence, or it is going to give me a new chance to change my life. Maybe being away from my old life will give me the chance to get away from the nightmares.

I zone out listening to the accents surrounding me. The cold air is whisking through my hair, being at a new school in the middle of the school year is hard, everyone already has friends, I missed the freshman orientation. My roommate was less than thrilled seeing me arrive, thinking she was going to be able to go all freshman year without a roommate.

I open my eyes looking around me, the courtyard is full of students. The walkways are stone covered by large trees. The best part of all: there is no snow. There is a bulletin board in the centre of the courtyard where all the walkways meet. Gardens are scattered everywhere, waiting for spring. The smell is almost as unsettling as New York with car fumes lingering in the air.

I drop my cigarette into the ashtray and venture off into the fine arts building, ready to take on my first day.

I eye down an art easel that is right next to the big open window. Distracted, I walk into class with a group of people trying to fit through the door at the same time. I fight through the crowd and sit down gazing at the view of the campus, hoping my inspiration can finally come from anything other than the burning hate that burns deep down in my belly.

"I am Mr Allen." He scans the classroom. "We are working today with charcoal."

I knew the accents were going to be hard to get used to, that's not the part that's hard for me. It's hard not to get lost in what everyone is saying. I could sit here and listen to everyone say the most random words and I would be lost forever.

Music starts to play from the speakers, I can feel myself becoming lost in my own world of art.

It isn't until the music shuts off and I look at the art piece in front of me. I need some counselling or some happiness in my life. The demon that is looking back at me is going to be raising a lot of questions. The assignment was to draw how you see yourself.

I breathe through my lips making them vibrate, I'm going to be deported back to the states faster than I can blink. If I can control my mind when I start to draw, I would. The only way I stay sane is from the connection of my mind to my hand, without it, I would be lost. My thoughts would never be released.

I pick up a cloth from the easel wiping the black from my fingers. My work is actually really good, hopefully, Mr Allen sees it this way too. Art is about pulling your layers back. It just so happens that I haven't been able to peel enough layers back to see the good in me.

I glance around the classroom looking at everyone around me. Everyone has broken off into their own conversations, leaving me as the odd man out. It wouldn't be so bad if I was used to being alone every once in a while. All of us back home were clingy, we held onto each other with dear life.

"Interesting." Mr Allen's voice is low standing behind me. "Explain it."

I look at it wide-eyed. "I wish I could."

"I see the urge to change."

"I see a starving artist."

"We all are, that's why I teach." He chuckles before walking away. "We are going to get along nicely."

Great, my only friend is a teacher. Loser alert.

***

Lunchtime, the dreadful debate about sitting alone or smoking the hunger away.

I stand in the line-up digging through my wallet for my student ID card. I grab a tray setting it on top of the glass sliding it across, careful not to judge the food in front of the cooks. Trying not to eavesdrop on conversations is almost impossible, especially when you are dying to be a part of them. My tray is being loaded with vegetables and questionable meat. I place an orange juice on my tray while swiping my card. Walking to the back corner of the room sitting at the edge of the table, half hoping and half dreading someone sitting next to me.

"Boys are the death of me." The girl from this morning with the auburn sits a few chairs down with her arms crossed leaning into the table. She looks up at her friend. "Bastards."

She rolls her eyes picking at her food. Her short auburn hair, green-grey eyes and round face are oddly beautiful. I look up at her friend and pucker my lips together. She is my roommate, the same dormmate who was less than thrilled to have me around.

She looks up and her brown eyes shoot daggers at me. "Hayley," She says simply.

I press my lips in forcing a smile.

It only takes a few seconds to have their friends gathered at the table. The voices and bodies surrounding me are making me feel claustrophobic. I've spent most of my life wishing I was invisible, now that I am invisible, I wish someone would see me. I pull out my phone searching Spencer's social media. The last picture he shared was the eight of us sitting around; we all have a drink in one hand and a cigarette in the other. My body feels hollow looking at all their faces.

I stuff my phone back into my purse fighting the urge to break down and cry. I knew moving was going to be hard, I just underestimated how hard it was going to be. My food was barely touched before they all piled around me making me feel insignificant. I stand up pushing out my chair, still, no one bothers to look over at me. I walk to the garbage can behind me, dumping my tray.

I walk over to the door and out to the courtyard. I need a smoke. I also need to remind myself how long it took me to do my makeup this morning. My eyes are watering over, I take a step and my body jolts into someone.

I glance up looking at a guy who is taller than I am. His eyes are a light aqua colour, with perfectly styled hair. I look away, stepping to the side. "I'm sorry."

Archie

Who is this girl and where did she come from? Her American accent takes me off guard. "It's okay." She's already long gone. I'm talking to the bricks where her feet once stood.

I look in the direction she is walking, she is standing in the middle of the path looking into her handbag. Her hands are shaking. I don't know who she is, but her perfume is still lingering in the air around me. She never batted her eyes when she saw me, it's refreshing. She didn't look at me and became speechless like every other airhead at this university. Her eyes were dark; I only looked in them for half a second, her soul was crying for help.

I place my fag between my lips. That was too fucking poetic for me.

"Eh Mate. You listening?" Ron waves his hand in front of my face.

I raise my eyebrows wrinkling my forehead.

"Marissa is coming, I tried to warn you."

She rolls her eyes when she sees me mumbling "Bastard" under her breath.

She likes to pretend she hates me, our Mum's have been best friends forever. We have known each other since we were both in diapers. She knows every deep dark monster that lives deep inside me.

I put my hand out wrapping my arm around her waist. I am a dick after all. I know she likes me and I toyed with that, it just wasn't there for me. We connect on a different level. She might be okay being dragged into my life, I'm just not okay pulling her into it.

"Who's the American?" I shouldn't be asking her about another girl after our failed date. I nod my head towards the long brown-haired siren.

Marissa swats me away taking the fag away from my fingertips. "No idea."

"She's my roommate." Ava looks at the siren with squinted eyes.

Ava is useless, and a bitch. She might come in handy for the first time.

"She cries a lot."

"I'd cry a lot if I lived with you too." Ron mumbles.

I try to stiffen a laugh. I look over my shoulder looking at her upturned serene eyes. She takes a drag off her fag talking on her phone. A single tear runs down her face and I'm fighting every urge to go save her.

What the hell is wrong with me?

I drop my hand from Marissa's waist, "Go make friends with her."

"I'm not going to be your wingman!" She sounds offended, I can't blame her.

I smile smugly looking at Ron, he looks as shocked as I feel. "I don't need a wingman."

"You will when she finds out about your dark secret."

"What dark secret?" Ava crosses her arms. "No one tells me anything."

Ron slaps his knees. "That's the end of this conversation."

I back away. "Dinner and drinks at Bell."

Bell is the closest pub to the girl's dorm, neither of them drive and the food isn't half-bad. If people from school go out, that is the place they go to. Locals only go there if it's between semesters or the summer months.

Crossing my fingers, hoping that maybe my siren will be there.

Chapter 2

Hayley

My roommate left almost an hour ago, not like I was expecting her to tell me where she was going and I definitely wasn't expecting an invite. Trying to find a place to eat close to the dorms has been almost impossible. There is one pub around called Bell and it has been my go-to every single day since I have been here. The dorm is right in the middle of a neighbourhood and I am too lazy to make myself food. At least my bank account allows me to eat out whenever I feel like it.

Bells is red, the same shade of red as London phone booths. It's tall, even though it's one floor. The inside is packed full of tables and I recognise a lot of students from school pilled in.

The same server, who has worked for the past five nights I've come in here, passes me a bag and the debit machine, already used to my routine. I have no idea what the custom amount to tip is here, I'm probably over tipping. I set down the debit machine and walk away.

"If I'm going to pretend to be your mate, we may as well be mates."

I turn around looking at the same girl who is friends with my roommate Ava. "He saw right through you. I really hope you're not taking acting classes."

She frowns. "Eh. I am."

I scrunch my nose, unsure if there is a point in getting myself out of it or not.

"He? Boyfriend?"

I laugh through my nose, it's so nice talking about Josh without girls swooning over him. "One of my brothers."

"Come sit."

I'm taken off guard mostly because I wasn't expecting her to talk to me, let alone invite me to eat with her. I don't know how to make friends outside of the tightly knit friend group. I look over her shoulder and Ava is sitting in the booth. I grunt.

"She had the same reaction, just come on."

I nod, following her to the table. As much as I don't want to be alone, sitting with my miserable roommate is better than nothing.

I get up to the table and Ava moves her round body looking up at me brushing her shoulder-length hair onto her back. She looks less than pleased that I am here, I can't blame her. Being around her feels like the last little bit of life I have deep down within myself is fading away.

I stand there awkwardly rocking onto my heels. Is it too late to walk away?

One of the guys look over at me, he is the same one I accidentally ran into at lunch. He looks up at me pausing and then looks away.

Rude.

A guy beside him smacks his arm. "I'm Ron, and before you ask, no, not Ron Weasley. That's Marissa and Archie's the arsehole beside me."

"I'm really not that bad." Archie looks up at me flashing me a smile.

His deep British accent is sending my mind into overdrive. I never noticed it earlier, his face is damn close to perfection. The worst part is, he knows it. But little does he know, I'm immune to attractive guys.

He scoots over enough in the booth allowing enough room for me and my takeout containers to sit next to him.

Ava slouches in the booth, she looks so uncomfortable and I am in no place to feel unwanted. I already have to deal with that at the dorm, I don't want to feel like that right now and then all night too. My chest aches, I finally had the chance in almost a week not to be alone. I pull my eyes from her, taking a step backwards. "I'm just going to head back to the dorms, thanks though."

"Do you need a ride?" Archie's aqua eyes are cutting into me like he's trying to read me.

"It's only a few blocks."

Archie

I watch her walk away from me, I don't understand it. I don't chase after girls. Girls chase after me. I don't even know her name, but damn the sadness in her voice is enough to piss off the gods.

"Why are you sending Marissa to talk to her when you know very well that she likes you?" Ava sneers.

I look over at Marissa, she is biting down on a chip watching my reaction. Fuck, I'm a bigger dick than I thought

I was. Our friendship comes first and Marissa knows that. She has always had a crush on me, and I thought why not see if anything is there? We never even made it to the kissing part of our date, it was awkward for the both of us. We are both lucky that we can sit at the same table or be around each other still.

Marissa smirks watching me squirm. "It's fine."

"That's what every girl says before hell freezes over." Ron shakes his head. "It's never fine."

"This time it's fine though. She insulted my degree, says I can't act."

"So, we don't like her?" Ava rests her elbow on the table picking at the food on the plates.

"No, we like her, for now." Marissa looks at me.

I never ask permission to do anything in life, she knows that. She is my best friend, her opinion matters. She also knows that I never ever end up on this side of a chase. Ron pats my back, and my mind is made up. I'm setting aside my demons and going to let her in. It is going to take a lot of work. She never bats an eye around me. Charming her isn't going to work. For the first time in my life, I need to be a nice guy.

***

The sun is barely awake. The streets of London are slow, in only an hour, cars are going to be out, and the streets will be packed. The city will have no idea what has happened, but I will. I will because I was the one to inflict the pain.

I park my car on the side of the street, just outside of an abandoned warehouse. I'm half-shocked that the police haven't caught on to us coming and going. As much as I wish

18

they wouldn't catch on, I find myself also wishing they could catch on so we can be free of this mess. Even life in prison would feel a hell of a lot better than this.

I open the door listening to voices, I have no idea what is happening, only that it's urgent. I can hear my Dad's chatter. He's yelling at someone. "You are going to get us caught!"

"The police already know about us, Alfie. It's just a matter of time before they arrest you and work their way down."

"They are going to arrest us because you sent them tips!"

My heart speeds up, beating so loudly I can only hear that and the blood pulsing through my ears. I take back all my thoughts, I don't want to spend life in prison. I open the door slamming it against the wall. My dad has a gun in his hands, it's already cocked. He's just too scared to shoot his best friend and end it all.

I take the gun from his hands pointing it at Jeremy's head, ignoring the pleading in his green eyes, I pull the trigger. My body goes stiff watching life pull from him. His body hits the ground hard with blood pouring out from the bullet wound in his head.

Dad takes the gun from my hands. My ears are still ringing. His face has fear written all over it. He knows he destroyed me. I never even hesitated, it wasn't the first time I've killed and it sure won't be the last time I'll kill someone. My hand used to shake, I used to feel sick about it. Somewhere down the line, I stopped feeling as guilty.

"I turned you into a monster." Dad rubs his forehead.

My father is the only Cartel boss with a heart. I don't know how he has been balancing it for fifteen years, but somehow he has been doing it. This is the first time I've ever had to make the kill because he couldn't bring himself to do it. He is going to make sure it is the last.

Even with him raising me as a mobster, he was a good dad. He hid this life from me until he thought I could handle it. I accidentally stumbled upon it when I was seventeen, since then I've been sucked in. My life and every decision I have made has revolved around the Baker Cartel.

Ignoring his comment. "Do you need me to help deal with the body?"

"Go to school. I'll deal with the cops if they come around, let me know."

I nod even though we both know they won't. I have my Mums last name and they were never married. He owns a house in his name, and she owns one in her name. He has done everything in his power to keep this life separate from family. He has never once showed up to any of my school events and with good reasoning. Growing up knowing my parents were together but lived in separate houses was confusing.

Like I said, he's a good man. I mean, other than the killing and being the ringleader of a cartel.

I walk out of the building, the sun has woken up and the streets are busy. The entire city has no idea of the life I just stole. No one other than the Baker Cartel will know. His family will be concerned, debating about placing a missing person report. Then they will realise that no one else is missing the mobster but them. They might fight for a funeral, but Jeremy's body will magically disappear. Almost making a funeral impossible to happen.

I race down the street in my car trying to ignore all the pain I inflicted without missing a single breath.

Chapter 3

Hayley

My head hurts from crying all night. I'm so mentally drained being away from everyone. I never thought this through, I never thought any of this through. I was so worried about running from the demons in my life, I never second-guessed what it was going to be like to face every single day without the people I love.

I hear my name being called, I look behind me, Ron is standing beside Archie waving. I have no idea if people are normally like this when they try to make new friends or if I am just making it that obvious that I'm lonely. I pop a cigarette into my mouth walking around a crowd of people.

Archie looks up towards me, giving me a weak smile. There's a darkness in his eyes, it's fear. I recognise it from the mirror. He laughs once before hauling a drag of his smoke. "You have two choices, you can go hang out alone in your dorm. Or you can stand here with us and insult Marissa's awful acting."

I press my lips together trying to fight off a smile.

"This is what? Our third conversation and you finally smiled?"

I can feel my cheeks burn. I'm not going to give him the satisfaction of watching me squirm. Every game he has in the book I've seen. I hang around seven dangerously attractive guys, I know it all.

I look him straight into his aqua blue eyes. "That wasn't a real smile."

"Challenge accepted."

I roll my eyes as he puts his lighter up to my cigarette. I'm flattered that he is taking time to try to make me smile, he just won't know that. Ron and Archie erupt in laughter, I'm too busy staring at the burning cherry, and I never heard what was so funny.

"You're coming over this weekend, right?" Archie tips his head ever so slightly.

I raise my eyebrows. "You don't want me hanging around, I promise you."

Archie is looking at me unfazed. It's like he's bored even.

Ron shoves him to the side. "He won't take no for an answer."

"What if I have to study?"

"I have beer," Archie says deadpanned like it's going to convince me otherwise.

I scrunch my nose. "I'm more of a straight-up whiskey kind of girl."

Archie raises his eyebrows, and his eyes are wide. "Do all Americans have drinking habits of forty-year-old men?"

I drop my head looking down at the ground smiling, a real smile. I look up at him watching him admire me. "Just me and my friends." I shrug. "I'm only here for this semester, you may as well show me a good time."

"You're only here for one semester?"

"Unless you want to marry me, yup."

He pulls his lips to the side then shakes his head twice, like he is considering it.

"I was kidding! I have to go to class."

"Before you go." He pulls out his phone, handing it to me to an empty contact.

I put my number in, Ron is watching me. I don't know if that shocked look is his permanent facial expression, but it's the one he always wears when I'm around. I take a step back heading towards the fine arts building.

Archie points behind me. "That's the arts building!"

I raise my hands to my shoulders shrugging.

He starts to laugh, his smile showing off his perfect white teeth is enough to make me smile in return. "Bloody hell, I might need to marry you so you can survive."

I spin on my toes, turning around laughing. For the first time in a week, I've laughed and smiled because I was happy, not just faking it. Damn it, he reminds me of everyone I left back home. He is going to be a good friend to keep around.

***

It feels like the rest of the week happened so fast that everything turned into a blur. Before I know it, I'm getting ready to go to Archie's, well not really getting ready. More like sitting on my bed drawing, waiting for time to pass. I need a drink. I went from having a drink every single day to not having one for two weeks.

I'm outside. My phone lights up to a text from Archie.

There's a pounding at my door, I grab my purse. Ava is notorious for forgetting her key. One more thing I can't stand about her. I stand up dragging my long legs to the door swinging it open.

Archie is standing in front of me with his hands in his sweater pockets. "I thought it would be more gentlemanly of me to come and get you."

"How did you get in here without an escort?"

He steps to the side to reveal Ava. "I forgot my key."

I blink four times, fighting down everything I want to say to her.

"Come on, let's go." Ava shoves past me.

Both Archie and I sigh, at the exact same second.

I pull the door shut, turning the lock. "This is going to be fun," I mumble under my breath.

"I know, just ignore her. I do." He puts his hand on the arch of my back.

He is exactly like everyone I left back home. Even the smallest gesture is taking me back to everyone. My heart sinks, I didn't know it was humanly possible to miss people this much. I take a few giant steps forward to get out of his reach.

My phone rings with Dillon's name light up, this kid always has the perfect timing. I walk down the stairs, looking behind me. Archie is far enough back he won't hear Dillon on the other line and Ava is nowhere to be seen.

"Dillon," I say breathlessly. "I miss you."

"I miss you too." He's drunk, I can almost smell the whiskey over the ocean.

"It's eleven am there. Why aren't you at school? This is your senior year."

"I'm drunk because we all miss you. Liam is a whore. You broke his heart," He hiccups. "You broke his heart years ago, he just thought there was a chance for you guys to get back together."

"Where have you been getting this much alcohol from?"

"I moved in with Liam and William. Dad is out of control."

I open the door standing off to the side looking at Archie, I stick my finger in the air to say one minute silently. I move my hand covering my mouth and the mouthpiece to block out the wind from carrying my words. "Why?"

"He's on a death mission, I swear. He is on a hunt to find you. You can't just leave the Basilisks."

"Get some sleep, get Spence or Josh to call me later. Goodnight."

"I miss you."

The line disconnects. My stomach is turning, making me nauseous, the colour has faded from my face. I feel dead, my body is numb. Martin is going to find me and he's going to kill me with no hesitation. It doesn't matter that his son loves me or that I will always be in love with his son. It's doesn't matter that my birth father and Josh's dad are his followers. It doesn't matter that I'm friends with his follower's children or that his nephew is my best friend. None of that fucking matters to this relentless Mafia boss. He only wants blood.

It just so happens that my name is on his hit list.

Feeling scared is the understatement of the year. I am petrified. I know what the Basilisks are capable of, I know that because I am one of these ruthless gangsters. I pull up my sweater looking down at my arm, my cover-up is doing a perfect job at hiding my tattoo of a black and grey snake that states I am one of them. Too bad, the cover-up doesn't make me invisible.

I really hope my relationships with everyone are strong enough for them to keep where I am a secret.

Archie

The house I own is my greatest priced possession. I paid it out, with filthy money. I can't tell people I own it because what kind of twenty-one-year-old university student owns a fucking house? I love bringing people over, everything is modern and up-to-date. Everyone but Hayley seems to be impressed by it.

I could start flying and she wouldn't even notice.

Why the hell am I so wrapped up in her?

Don't think I didn't notice, ever since she got off the phone she has a look of fear in her eyes, it is pretty close to the look Jeremy had before I shot him in the head earlier this week. I want to ask what's wrong, she's too strong for her own good.

She's dangerous, everything about her is fucking dangerous.

I walk into the living room pulling a bottle of whiskey from the cupboard, bought just for her. It's a single malt and fucking expensive so she better at least enjoy it, or say thank you. "Si—" I pause, blinking hard, I almost called her Siren. "Hayley, come here."

I look past her, she is standing brushing her hands against the soft leather couch. Ron is laughing into his hand.

Hayley looks up at me, I move my head telling her to come.

I pour a cup making sure it's in her line of sight. Her smile is broken. She reaches for the cup with shaky hands chugging it back, she's holding the cup out asking for more.

I pour her cup half full. "Go easy, I don't need you to be crashing in my bed tonight." *I'm not kidding.*

She puts the cup to her lips, tipping it back while taking a small drink. "Don't worry, I won't be. Thank you for this Arch."

I knew we got closer over the last few days, hearing her come up with a nickname for me is making me a little bit too happy.

"You alright?"

"Oh. Yeah, I'll be okay."

She spins around on her toes turning back into the living room, her long brown hair does a half-circle. She has a lot of hair. How am I supposed to do this? Fighting every nerve in my body to grab her hips and pull her against my dick, instead, I let her walk away. How am I supposed to be around a girl when all I want to do is lay her down in my bed and fuck her until she screams my name over and over? My eyes keep dropping down to her boobs, her bloody sweater keeps getting in the way.

It's like she can read my mind, she sets down her cup on the table and takes off her sweater. She's wearing a dark blue tank top with some kind of flower on the bottom corner. My eyes are drawn to her arms, she is covered in tattoos. Her right arm is a complete colourful sleeve. I'm aware I'm staring at her; I'm probably drooling too. She has more muscle on a girl than I've ever seen before. It's not overly a lot of muscle, you can tell she's tone and strong.

Usually seeing a girl like this is a turn-off, tattoos aren't my thing. A strong girl? No, thank you. I don't know if it's her, or if she's just screwing me up that much, but she's the definition of breath-taking.

"Archie." Melissa breaths my name. "Stop it."

Hayley looks up, she never saw me staring.

Ron groans. "Let's go out."

Both Ava and Melissa jump to their feet without second-guessing it. Going out is the last thing on my mind. By the looks of Hayley making herself comfortable on the couch, it's the last thing she wants as well.

"Archie, come on!" Ava stands behind Hayley.

Hayley looks at me rolling her eyes, it is going to kill Ava to pretend like Hayley is in the same room as her.

"I'm staying here. I could go for a movie." I walk to the bookshelf listening to the door slam.

"You can go with them. I can go home," Her voice is echoing into her glass.

"You can go with them too, but you're still here. I want a quiet night, with or without you."

"Put the damn movie in."

I grab the first thing I see, not even paying attention to what it is. At least she's here with me. As long as I keep my distance from her, we can stay just as friends, and then she won't walk away from me. I can keep her away from the dark side in me.

My dark side hasn't been as bad since she has walked into my life. Somehow Siren has changed everything without even trying. It hasn't even been a week since she bumped into me, the light behind her dark serene eyes acts like a lighthouse for me to find my path in life. She is the lightest part of my life and I don't even know anything about her.

Chapter 4

Hayley

I bat my thick fake eyelashes. My mind hits a second of confusion. I can't remember where I am. I pull the blanket up farther. This is the comfiest bed I have ever had the chance to lay on. Archie cologne is strong on the sheets, on the comforter and probably seeped into the mattress. I wasn't even drunk last night, I must have fallen asleep watching the movie. The fear, anxiety, adrenaline and the little bit of alcohol in my system took a toll on me.

I roll over, his cologne is probably only this strong because he is sleeping next to me but he isn't here. The mattress is still cold to touch, he never stayed in his bed last night.

I lay on my back looking at the roof, trying to listen for any noise in the house. I've experienced gentlemen for myself, it's one of the codes in the Basilisk Mafia, experiencing it without expecting it, is completely different. This is an amazing feeling, even though I know that wasn't his intention and I'm never going to get this again. It still feels really fucking nice.

I sit up in bed looking down at my arm, the cover-up has almost completely faded on my tattoo. I look to the side and my hoodie is sitting on the end table with my phone on top of it and a sticky note stuck to my phone. *I had to deal with something. There's tea in the cupboard by the fridge.*

A text message would have been fine, but the thought of him writing a handwritten note is about a thousand times better. Archie probably has girls lining up outside his house right now, either that or he is taken, when you look like that and do things like this you are not staying single for long.

Which means, I need to get out of another girl's boyfriends' bed right this instant.

My phone rings in my hand, I slide on my sweater. I gasp looking down, fumbling with the phone. "Spence! Why are you awake?"

"I couldn't sleep. Cameron had to talk me down all night." He pauses. I hear him take a shaky breath; I can imagine the hurt in my brother's eyes. His girlfriend is probably lying next to him walking him through this call. "Why are you on our hit list?"

I take a deep breath looking at the blank cream colour wall ahead of me. If I say one thing wrong to any of them, they are going to go to Martins and blow the place up. "I will handle it. Don't tell him where I am."

"Of course, I won't. None of us will Hayley. How the fuck are you going to handle this?"

"I don't know. I'll come to New York during Easter Break, if he wants to kill me, he can do it himself. This is what I get for running away, I dug my own grave."

"Listen, Liam has a plan. It won't be for a while. He is refusing to tell anyone but you. We might be making a trip."

"Go to bed big brother, I love you."

"I love you, baby sister."

I hang up the phone, falling back on the bed. Spencer and Josh are both only a year older than I am, we are closer than any brother and sister should be.

Liam having a plan is going to be a nightmare. He is the most emotionally screwed up person I know. I was dating him off and on from the time I was six, up until two years ago. Since then he has spent his time numbing the pain of sleeping around with the entire campus. He won't give up and date someone just in case there is a sliver of hope for us.

I know that nothing is there, there hasn't been anything there for a long time. I love him and I always will, it's just my love for him has turned into more of an unconditional family love. I'm ready to move on, he's still stuck in the past.

Out of everyone, I had the most screwed up childhood. Mine and Josh's mom died six years ago. Josh even had a normal uprising. The one thing that all eight of us have in common is that we have been getting primed for this since we were children. At the age of sixteen, we all became gangsters. They were bred to be Basilisks, I was the mistake Basilisk. Normally girls don't make the cut, unfortunately, I did. I grew up as one of the boys, I would beat them in fights and my target practice is just shy from perfect.

I wish we had memories of travelling, or family events. Every single memory we have is of each other. We were Basilisks long before it was official. Even if our mom's wanted to save us from it, it was impossible. We couldn't leave the country without it being "work" official.

And that is why I am on a hit list. It's not an official rule, it's an unspoken one. Only those who are stupid enough to find themselves are the ones strong enough to fight back.

I'm ready to fight Martin, for the first time in my life I have seen more of the world and that is something worth fighting for. For now, I am going to sit here and look forward to seeing whoever comes with Liam to see me.

Looking forward to seeing them is the one thing I can control. If Martin takes the life out of me, I can't control that, but I can live life until he does.

"Siren. Bloody…Hayley."

Did Archie just call me siren? I get off his bed with light feet walking out his bedroom and down the stairs. "Did you just call me a siren? Do you think I layer ships to an island to kill them? Or am I just that fucking annoying?"

He turns around dropping a bag onto the living room coffee table. "You're an enchantress. You enchant people."

I sit down to pull a Marlboro from my pack from the couch popping one in my mouth and tossing another to Archie. "Careful, if your girlfriend hears you talk like that, you'll be in trouble."

I'm normally good at reading people's emotions. He puzzles me, it kind of infuriates me. He lights his cigarette staring me down. Do I change the conversation? What do I do?

He falls on the couch right beside me pulling his ashtray on his lap. "There's no one in this town for me."

I push out a laugh. I am insulted, maybe he's one of those gay people that you can't tell is gay. Dillon's like that. "Are you gay?"

The words left my mouth, and he bursts out in a belly laugh. He's waving his hand around trying to breathe. "You're a funny mug. I'm not bloody gay. Eat your bacon, before you make me do something, I'll regret eh?"

His accent makes my knees weak. "Can you just talk all day? Just random words."

I lean forwards, his torso brushes against my back, his mouth is dangerously close to my ear. "I like your American accent too, but you're going to lose it soon, mug. Then when you leave me all the boys will be asking you to talk."

Shivers run all over my body, goosebumps are raised on my skin in places that I never knew was possible. "I don't chase boys. Actually, I don't chase at all."

"My mum puts on a big ball, it's not till March. Still, two months away, do you want to be my date?"

I pass him a container without checking what is in it. "If by the date you mean as friends?"

"Friends. You just have to save me one dance."

"You have yourself a friend date."

Archie

Friend date? What the hell is that? I've been friend-zoned. Either I need to work really fast or the regret of me not working hard enough before she moves back to New York is going to eat me alive. I need to come up with something intimate for her to see me. I mean, really see me, she needs to see past my trash I pack around. I need her to see me as the person that lives deep down within me.

I'm not sure who lives there, all I know is he digs himself out more and more each time she is around.

"Mate. You're shaking." Ron passes me a cup of water.

I put my hands on my head leaning my elbows into my thighs. I had to kill today, I had to skip classes to do a job. I don't even know who he was. I haven't been this bothered by the cartel since I was a teenager. "She's bloody destroying me, Ron."

The person who tries to dig up when she's around has been resurfacing more and more, the devil inside me is fading away. With her leaving, that is the worst possible thing imaginable.

"Blow her off for a while." Ron shrugs like it's the easiest thing in the world. "If Alfie finds out you've gone soft mate, he will kill her."

"What if we kill Alfie? We could be free."

Ron looks at me like I've gone mad. "You can't kill your father, you do and a new boss steps up. It's a never-ending circle." He snorts. "If it could work we'd be free."

"It's a bad idea. I can't stay away from her. I need to keep her safe."

***

Four days. That's how long I have managed to stay away from Siren. Four dreadful bloody days. I can't take it anymore. The devil inside me is breaking through, she can't go back to New York at the end of the semester. Being away from her is like eating a poisonous prickly thorn.

People volunteer to feel like this why? I stay far away from anyone or anything that can cause emotion. People die, and they die frequently. Of course, a lot of that death is inflicted by me or any other member of the Baker Cartel. She feels safe, I know she isn't as stupid as I am to stumble across a Cartel and be sucked in.

She is standing on the pathway of the courtyards talking to someone, I don't recognise him. A burning sensation is in

34

the pit of my belly. I want to rip his eyes out of his head for giving her the time of day. He's making her laugh.

Oh hell no.

My feet are carrying me towards her, no one should be making her laugh except for me. Her eyes are twinkling, for the first time since I've seen her she looks genuinely happy. Am I going to take that from her? Probably, I'm a living nightmare.

I pull the Marlboro from her stained fingers. "Who's this?" The burning in my belly is being projected in my tone. I have no right to sound like a jealous douchebag.

She twists her head towards me, her eyes beaming with what I imagine to be close to hatred. "This is Jason." His eyes lights up and a small smirk spread across her face.

I missed her smile, I missed being the reason for her smile. I extend my hand to shake his. "Alright mate?"

He blushes, touching my hand lightly shaking it. He lets go and walks away, not saying anything.

Jason is out of sight and Hayley laughs harder than I ever heard a girl laugh after encountering a jealous arsehole. She turns to me, the laughter stops. She gives me a shove on the shoulders, making a big scene. "You are a dick. You do know that right? One, he's liked you since the start of the year. Two, you can't ignore me then march over here like I'm your fucking property."

How can I not laugh? She's adorable when she's mad.

"Damn it, Arch! I'm mad at you. Why is this funny?" Her accent is starting to come through. Even though it's only been a few weeks, she is starting to sound less and less like a New Yorker.

"Next time he might not be gay."

"Good. A girl has needs." She pulls another fag from her pack, lighting it. Her voice is full of irritation, I really can't blame her.

I look dumbfounded, it hasn't even registered in her beautiful brain, she has no idea that I have fallen for her. She's going to go back to New York, and she will never know. I need to think of something fast. "Draw me." The words slip out of my mouth.

"You haven't even seen my work."

"I don't care. Draw me. Use it for an assignment for something."

I wanted to be intimate. Maybe this way I can see how she sees me. That's a thing, right? Your peer into an artist's mind through their work? I'm so out of my league here, she deserves better than the heartless monster I am. The gears behind her eyes are working hard.

"Let me paint you instead. Arch, please don't be offended if it turns out bad. I've never done a person before. I don't want you to think I see you differently than I do."

Does she care about me? Or is she saying if it's good, she doesn't want me to look into it as her having feelings for me? My head hurts, girls suck.

"When do you want to do it?"

"It's going to have to wait till this weekend. If you are free. I don't know how long it's going to take."

"My schedule is always clear for you, Siren." I snap, forgetting part of the reason Marissa sent me to find her. "Dress shopping after school. Marissa needs you to come to Ava, she says everything looks good."

Her smile makes the sunshine brighter. "I might steal your best friend."

She walks past me placing her hand on my arm, offering me a smile as she walks by. Anyone else could look into her eyes and see nothing, when I look into them, I see a darkness that I am all too familiar with. I never told her this, I'm really unsure if I should. When she stayed at my place on Friday, she was having some pretty gruesome nightmares.

Something happened to her in America, I will move heaven and earth to find out what it is.

Hayley

Dress shopping sounds like torture. I'm keeping Dillon on speed dial so he can pick for us. I chose art as my getaway from the Basilisks, he chose fashion. Without a degree or any education, he is the most talented uncertified fashion stylist I know. He has saved me many, many times.

Even three thousand miles away, Dillon is going to be my saviour.

I can still feel the electricity bursting through my body since I touched Archie's arm, it's been hours and I can still feel him. I can still smell his cologne. Those four days he was avoiding me were painful. He never even made it discreet. He would see me and walk away. I would be talking with Jason and he would stand and approach another group, when I walked away.

I was scared that I scared him off with my nightmare Friday night. It was a flashback of me tossing a grenade into a building. It was the same night I almost killed Erik and Adam, I was sixteen. It was my first Basilisk job. The dream was twisted into Martin taking my name off his hit list. I woke up before my body crashed into the ground. My mind has been replaying the sound of his black-market handgun in my head since I woke up Saturday morning. Four years later, Erik still hasn't forgiven me for almost blowing him and his brother up. He pretends like he doesn't know me, I'm used to being ignored. He is one of the best guys I know, I guess it just makes it a little more painful when he's your best friends' brother.

The entire four days that Archie spent avoiding me gave my mind a lot of time to think. He is the first guy other than Liam that I have ever had feelings for. I can never think about unfriend-zoning him if that's even a thing. I'll be dead before our relationship has time to grow. That will only leave him heartbroken. He deserves so much better than to be wrapped up with a Gangster.

I have to encourage him to date, maybe even find a real date to this ball. I don't want to, but if that means I need to help him live once I'm dead, I'll do it. How am I supposed to paint him and not have him see the way I look at him?

Marissa walks out of the change room, pulling me away from my thoughts. She is in a lime green silk dress. I snap a picture including her puzzled face. I haven't told her about my help in America yet.

I sent the picture, in a blink, Dillon texts back. *She looks like a fucking turtle. How do you guys dress yourselves? She needs something orange and short. You need the same dress but bright red.*

I look up at her, her hands are on her hips. "Dillon says you look like a turtle."

I stand up, looking over the racks of designer clothes.

"At least he's honest," Marissa mumbled. "What am I looking for?"

"You need orange and short, probably like knee-high. I don't know. I apparently need that dress in red."

"Archie is buzzin' about you going with him, you know that right?"

I look down, pulling a reddish, orange dress off the hanger. Ignoring my fluttering heart. "It's just as friends. I kind of want to find him a real date, I can just go as your date, or Ava's even."

I glance over at Ava. She pulls her lip up in disgust. I really wish I knew what she hated about me so much. Not that I care.

"You are going with Archie."

I pass her the dress, taking a red one from her hands. "He's my best friend here, I don't want to hold him back. I'm not going to be here forever, he may as well get used to me being gone now."

Marissa rolls her eyes walking away. "You don't pay any attention."

Ava grunts. "Just get changed so we can go, eh?"

I walk to the change room, holding the curtain with a tight grip, I yank it open. "Why are you even here?"

"Not because I want to be. Everything looks the same."

Now it is time for me to roll my eyes. I close the curtain taking my clothes off, this is the first dress I've tried on. With my best friend's help, it's going to be a hell of a lot easier to get out of here. I pull the dress up, thankfully I was thinking and did some cover-up on the bullet holes in my arms. The dress has a cowl neckline, I only know that because the tags say so. The colour is bright red, just as if I cut into a watermelon.

I look jaw-dropping hot. I haven't worn anything like this since I moved, now that it isn't in my dress code to dress up at all times, I take serious advantage of baggy hoodies and jeans. I snap a picture in the mirror, sending it to Dillon.

I can hear Marissa and Ava talking in whispers. I pull open the curtain and Marissa's eyes are beaming. I quickly take a picture of her and send it to Dillon.

If I wasn't gay, and if my brother wasn't in love with you I'd get with you. I did the impossible again.

I tap my fingers on the screen. *Oh, shut it. Thank you.*

"I don't know who this guy is, but he's magic." Marissa spins in a circle. The ruffles in the dress spin with her lifting up ever so lightly. She stops and pulls up her tube top. "Archie may be buzzin' now, wait till he sees you in that."

I scrunch up my nose feeling the silk under my palms. I can't stop thinking about what his touch is going to feel like in this dress. I can't stop wondering what his touch feels like in general.

Archie

My Mum only has my dad over once every few days, I don't know how they can manage to be away from each other so often. I am usually over here twice or three times a week, I try to come over as much as I can. I usually pull up in the driveway and get called away. I hate her face when she remembers what I do for a living, so I usually wait until my work for the day is done.

Her living room is filled with furniture that my dad bought her, everything in this house and including the house was bought with my dad's money. He is the reason they don't live together, it was only fair he supplied her with everything.

I sit on the couch watching my mother bring the tray with a teapot, and cups sitting on top of it over the tea-table. She was dying for a second baby. I remember her pleading with my dad for one. She couldn't understand why she couldn't have another one. I got older and she was still begging, then one day the begging stopped, and he moved out.

I'm not sure what happened. I think it has to do with when he became boss, he moved around the same time his father passed away. As I got older, I learnt his father was the Baker Cartel boss.

Mum sets the tray down smiling. Botox is her best friend, the thought of looking her actual age is too tragic. It's noticeable Botox, although I think it's noticeable on everyone who has it. No one says anything, she keeps getting more and she's happy. "What's her name?"

"What are you talking about?" I say deadpanned.

"You know exactly what I'm talking about."

"Hayley. She's an American student here for the semester." I tip my head back scrubbing my face with my hands. "I'm fucking friend-zoned mum."

She glares at me.

"Sorry."

"Tell her you love her, son."

"I don't love her. I'm not capable of loving someone."

She raises her hand, swatting me across the head. "I never raised you to think that. I had one chance at being a mum, you don't get to think that."

I put my hands up in front of me with my palms out. "Jesus."

"You are in love because you are sitting here telling your mom about her. Now get off my couch and tell her."

"I can't!" I hit my hands against the brown velvet couch. "Why would she love a cold heart murder? She's way too good for me. It actually makes me sick to my stomach."

My eyes travel around the living room, my dad has bought everything my mum needs plus more. She has a big-screen TV hanging from the wall, all her end tables are oak wood, the walls are painted a pastel blue. She has everything she needs, the only thing that is missing is her husband.

Hayley deserves more than this, she deserves to be loved by someone who can give her everything in the world. I sure as hell can, but only if money can pay for it. I can't promise the love and attention she deserves.

And she deserves a hell of a lot of it.

***

Calling Hayley and explaining to her to bring Marissa and Ava to dinner with my mum and Marissa's mum's was weird. My mum had this wild idea, she just had to meet her. It just so happened that the girls finished dress shopping. Who wants to go out for dinner with their friend's mum?

Hayley's long legs walk in, she's wearing high waisted pants with a tight long sleeve shirt. I never noticed hidden behind her baggy sweaters, her legs go on forever. Images of her legs wrapped around my waist flashes through my mind. I readjust hoping to hell I don't have to move from my booth for anyone to get in.

Siren hangs her purse and shopping bag on the coat rack by the booth, she doesn't pay attention to anyone else at the table. "Apparently, you will be 'Buzzin' When you see my dress. Whatever that means." She adds the quotation marks in the air.

She looks up, with her face turning beat red. "Oh my god. I'm sorry."

I grab her forearm, dragging her onto the booth to sit next to me. She lets out a small, almost silent squeak. I unwrap my fingers one, by one, just to test the waters. I brush my fingertips down her arm and over top of her hand. She doesn't pull away. I don't even care if she wants to.

Mum picks up her menu brushing her hand over it. "Hayley, you should really stay here longer, I'm sure you could get an extension."

I pull my hand away, embarrassed. My mum has made herself into my wingman.

Hayley gives a soft laugh. "It's tempting. I don't think I would like it here this much."

That wasn't directed towards me, but I'm going to take it. "You're welcome."

Ava huffs. "Archie and Marissa used to date."

Marissa picks up her menu hitting Ava's shoulder with it and I nearly choke on my own spit.

"Your point is?" I turn to look at Siren, she looks so unaffected. "I was thinking about getting Arch a real date instead of taking me to the ball." She turns to look at me. "What do you think?"

"Anything is better than a friend date."

She smiles scrunching her nose. "Exactly. I just remembered I have an assignment I have to work on. I'll see you guys at school tomorrow."

She grabs her shopping bag with the mystery dress in it off the coat rack and walks away without a second glance. What the hell just happened? Marissa and I went on one date. I want to chew Ava out, but I can hear Marissa already doing that. I'm too stunned to move, the one thing I was looking forward to going with her, she's replacing herself. Me stepping up my gentleman game hasn't worked, me trying to be friends with her sure as hell hasn't worked.

"I'm going home." I push myself out of the booth charging towards the door.

Marissa grabs my arm as I walk past. "I can take her as my date."

I look straight ahead, afraid to show that Siren is my weakness. I shake Marissa off and walk out of the restaurant.

Chapter 5

Archie

I was standing behind a wall for protection, then suddenly the next thing I knew I was standing in the line of fire like I had a fucking death wish. The doctors told me what bone it is, I just wasn't paying attention, nor did I care enough. This is my fourth time getting shot and the only time it has ever been bad enough to need to be at the hospital.

Trying to answer police questions when you are in a cartel is a bloody living fucking nightmare. The only words I could say were 'I don't know.' and 'they came out of nowhere.' I also threw in a few, 'I have no idea what they looked like, and I was too busy getting shot.'

Marissa has been the only visitor I've had. I was going crazy being stuck in there.

After I left Dinner my father called me in for an emergency hit, I never asked any questions. I just went in and started shooting. I was outnumbered and I blacked out trying not to remember anything that happened. Even if I wanted to answer the police's numerous questions, I wouldn't have been able to, I honestly don't remember a thing.

It feels like I've missed a week of school, it's only been three days so it might as well be a week. I am going to be so far behind. I have no idea why I'm walking to the arts building, my classes are in the complete opposite direction and Siren doesn't want to see me, she made that perfectly clear.

She is walking with her hoodie over her head hugging her sketchbook to her chest down the path to the arts building. I step down the stairs walking in her direction.

"Siren? Are you alright?" I use my good arm to touch her shoulder.

She looks up, her eyes are red and glossy. "Are we still on to do your painting tomorrow?"

I close my eyes, I forgot all about that.

"That's okay, I'll just use Jason and he can use me. I'm already late for class."

She tries to sidestep around me, I take one giant step to the side. "It's a project?"

She nods, her eyes locked on my chest.

I lean down, I missed her so much. My lips brush her cheek, I whisper in her ear, "I've had a lot going on in the last three days, just because I forgot doesn't mean I don't want you to do it."

Siren takes a deep breath. "I missed you."

I don't think I was supposed to hear those words leave her lips. She walks past me, I can tell her body is tense.

I turn around watching her leave, I know I heard her correctly. There was no mistake in what she said. Does she feel the same way? My god, I sure fucking hope so.

She stops turning around pulling the hood off her head. "You're my best friend, of course, I missed you."

Fuck. I give her a smile before walking away.

Hayley

Painting someone isn't even a project, I'm just dying to spend time with him. Running out on dinner because I felt threatened by Marissa was any girl's natural response. At least I thought it was, it might have been dramatic. It probably was dramatic. Then he fucks off to god only knows where for three days. I don't think I have much time left and as guilty as it makes me feel, I want to spend every last minute with Archie.

Feeling this way is unnatural. Especially when I feel this way and Liam isn't the recipient of my feelings. Archie has no idea how I really feel about him, I don't know what's more painful. The fact he may never know or the fact I need to watch him date someone else.

I don't know why I need to watch him date. It makes no sense to me, none of this does.

I place the blank canvas on top of the art easel, holding my paint pallet looking at the bandage on Archie's arm. I can't take my eyes away from it, I've seen it before. I shake my head, he wasn't shot. The life I ran away from is clouding my vision. I really didn't need him to take his shirt off, I could have painted him with his shirt on, this just feeds my dirty thoughts a tiny bit more.

My legs are weak and it's almost impossible to stand up. He doesn't have a single tattoo on his body, at least not one I can see. I kind of like it though, he is a blank canvas.

I dip my brush in the paint. I have never done this before, it's going to turn out horrible.

He is standing there with his arms crossed leaning against the wall. It's nothing special, so I can't figure out why he is taking my breath away. It might be because he is staring at me, I'm sure the building around us would fall and his vision would be locked on me.

"What was wrong yesterday?" His voice is gentle, almost like he's debating asking me.

Because I want to be with you, but I'm too dangerous and I don't want to put you in the line of fire. "Nothing, I was blinding."

He smiles with his eyebrows up. "You really are going to sound like you really are from London when you move back."

"Marry me and I won't have to." I laugh, poking fun is all I have right now.

"You suck at proposing."

"Good thing I wasn't proposing."

He quietly laughs.

The painting is going a lot smoother than I thought it was going to. Painting a person is a lot harder than I ever thought possible. No wonder a lot of tattoo artists refuse to do portraits. I have everything as close as I can to perfection. It's not perfect, but his abs are highlighted, his bulging arms are crossed making him look like a protector. His face is serious, everything that I love about him is showing in his light blue eyes. There is a small touch of white to show the sparkle in his eyes that I see. The man in the painting looks like someone that could save me. He looks like someone I love.

He can't see this. I pull the canvas off the easel. "I can't do people. I just wasted your Saturday."

Art has always opened my eyes to how I'm really feeling, I just never used it to know I'm in love. That's something I can't handle. I can't love him, he deserves to be loved by someone who isn't a monstrous murder.

He moves swiftly, pulling it out of my weak hands. His eyes are studying it intently. "This is how you see me?"

"I told you, it's shit."

"Don't find me a date." His voice is almost pleading.

"I need you to be okay when I leave."

"I can't believe you are making me do this." He places the canvas on the easel. He looks down at me and puts his hands on my shoulders. "What's your last name?"

"Cohen. How do you not know my last name?" I don't know his either, I'm not going to tell him that.

"Hayley Cohen, will you marry me, so my best friend doesn't have to leave?"

What the fuck is happening. I'm waiting for him to laugh or something. I love him, marriage is a way to save me. I just don't want it like this.

I use my right leg to lead me back a step. "Get on your knees."

I scrunch my nose watching him get down on one knee. He's actually serious.

"I can stay here all bloody night."

I smack his head. "You're unbelievable. I was kidding." I grab my purse, getting ready to leave.

He stands. "I'm not kidding. We need to at least try."

Why on earth am I considering this? Why is he willing to risk that for me? None of this makes sense. I have to try, maybe it will be my chance to save myself. "Fine."

"Wait what?"

Archie

How the bloody hell did that work? Not how I wanted it to go, I want her to marry me because she loves me. I want to scream. Mostly out of frustration, the woman of my dreams is going to be leaving in a few months and we are on our last chance of being together.

I raise my hand to my hair. "So, when do you want to move in?"

She starts laughing nervously, reflecting on how I'm feeling. Her eyes get wide and the laughter comes to a firm halt. "Never?"

"We have to be in love, remember?"

Her face turns white, I need to stop this before she passes out. "Siren, I'm just screwing with you. Go home. You aren't getting married."

"No. I-I need this. I can't say why. I just need this Arch, please."

Her eyes are clouding over, the strongest person I know. Stronger than I ever will be is crumbling before my eyes. I pull her in resting her head against my chest. Her body is trembling. I'm not ready to go to prison for the Cartel, but if it means I go to prison for trying to protect her. I won't hesitate. I won't regret it either.

"We will find a way alright future, Mrs Upton?" I had to toss my last name in there, I don't think she knew it.

As much as I don't want to, I pull away from her. I take her hand pulling her up the stairs to the bedroom. She can have my bed forever for all I care, it's a hell of a lot more comfortable than the spare bed. I stop in front of the door letting go of her hand. I walk straight to the room next to it.

"This is your room, you should have it." Her voice is low.

I can't look at her, when I do, the urge to kiss her gets stronger. I'm never going to get laid again since every female on campus will think we are in love. I'm still a guy and I can't get it from her. This is going to suck.

"If you stay in here, you're going to hate me in the morning."

"Then stay with me. If you want."

I take my shirt off over my head in the middle of the hallway, which was too obvious. I don't care. I walk into the room grabbing a pair of pants that are going to be way too big for her. She takes them from me walking to the bathroom.

I jump on the bed staring at the roof. I place my hand over my eyes. I fucked up. I just agreed to make her a Cartel wife. Real marriage or not, that's not something she deserves. I just need to end this, not only for me. I dragged Siren into this forgetting a huge factor.

I need to think of a way not to go to prison.

Chapter 6

Hayley

I remember waking up last night with tears soaking my face, I can't remember the dream. I woke up to Archie wrapping his arm around me pulling me into him. He even saves me from my unconscious mind, and he has no idea. I can't believe I agreed to make him a Mafia husband. Saving my life just to risk his makes zero sense to me.

The long sleeve shirt is chafing my arm, I need to find a better way to hide my snake tattoo. Everyone would take one look at us back home and know right away who we were. Me in my fancy dresses and the guys in suits twenty-four seven, it was a dead giveaway. Sidewalks would be cleared, everyone would get out of our way. We liked to pretend we hid it from everyone, we didn't. I have no idea how Erik has kept his police officer cover for so long.

Damn it, I need to call them. It's going to be midnight there, I have to wait a few hours. I can't chicken out.

I sit up from the bed holding my head. I can't believe I am so selfish I asked him to do this for me. He shouldn't have to live his life unhappily and protect me from my own dreams just because I ask him to.

"I made you coffee. It might taste like shit," Archie calls downstairs from the kitchen.

I shake my head smiling. The first time I came over here, he never even owned a coffee pot. He made me fall in love with him, he brought it on himself.

I put on my denim from yesterday. I walk over to his closet eying up his sweaters, trying to find the smallest thing in there. I never really paid attention until today, most of his clothes are red. No wonder he is going to be buzzin' when he sees my dress. I grab a black hoodie off the hanger and slip it over my head covering my long sleeve shirt.

I really need to learn British slang.

He's either not going to care I'm wearing his sweater, or he's going to lose his mind. Just another thing I stole from him.

I get in the kitchen to see creamer on the counter beside a coffee cup. He bought me four kinds not knowing which one I liked. I couldn't even imagine the confusion of a British person buying a coffee pot. I hope he knows I really appreciate it.

I look up at him staring at me. "I'll give you your sweater back after I stop at the dorms. I need to grab my things."

He walks up to me, he places his hand on my hips.

My heart is beating out of my chest having him this close to me.

His eyes drop down to my lips then back up to my eyes. "Keep it. I was thinking. If we want this marriage to not look like a sham, we need to act like we really are in love."

His voice deepens, if I didn't know better, I would say he is actually in love with me. His eyes are claiming me, he's intoxicating. His jaw is working under his skin. How is it possible to be this attractive?

He raises his hand to my face, his knuckles rubbing against my cheek. "It'll look like this."

His lips crash into mine with such force I almost lose my footing. His tongue caresses mine. I kiss him with every bit of willpower I have. My arms wrap around his middle pulling him in closer, his hands tangled in my hair. I let out a tiny moan, the sensitive parts of my body are tingling. He's kissing me like he owns me. I'm kissing him like he's mine. I feel his jeans rise against my sweater.

He pulls away. *How is that over? I need more!*

I walk to the coffee pot, I can feel the lust written all over my face. "That was pretty convincing."

"I'll give you a ride to the dorms to get your things."

***

Archie ran out in a panic. The school was weird, it was almost like he's never even dated a girl before. The looks I got were mixed with hate and jealousy. I took advantage of kissing him, he never seemed to mind. I am officially engaged to the hottest guy in the university. However the hell that happened.

The house is quiet. I'm sucked into the leather couch. This is the hardest phone call I've ever had to make. The guys are probably all together. I hope to God Erik isn't there, he is going to make me feel even shitter. I pick up the phone dialling Josh's number.

"Baby sister." I hear the echo as he puts me on speaker. Everyone said hi, I checked them off one by one and Erik's voice was nowhere to be found.

"Make sure you guys are sitting down."

William laughs. "You sound like a Spice Girl."

"I'm getting married."

"Fuck off. That's not funny." Liam's voice is beyond heartbroken.

"I'm on Martins fucking hit list, you guys. How the hell do I survive that? The way you guys work, I'm going to be at the top of the list in a few weeks."

"Does he at least love you?" Adam asks over to what sounds like Liam punching a hole in the wall.

Anger issues are nothing new between this group of guys. We've all had to replace walls a few times.

"No."

Everyone breaks off mumbling to themselves. Both of my brothers are silent. No one is offering me a better idea.

"Give me the phone." Liam scolds. I hear static as they pass me off, him stomping then his bedroom door shuts. "Hayley. Don't do this. We are supposed to end up together. Let me find a girl, I can get married and have kids. Baby, I'm already a Taylor. I can keep the boss bloodline going, I can be voted in as boss and end this for us."

My eyes are stinging with tears. Hearing him this upset is heart-wrenching. I will always love him, I can't ask him to bring another girl into this. Then add children to the mix. It doesn't matter what I say, he is going to do it.

"Hayley. Say something. I'm not capable of loving someone that isn't you. We both know that."

"Liam," I sniffle as a tear lands on my leg. How am I supposed to tell him I don't love him like that? We were toxic not only to ourselves but to everyone around us.

The front door opens, Archie has awful timing.

"He's there isn't he? Damn it, let me do this. I can do this. I will save you. I love you."

The line disconnects and I already know he is working on his master plan that will surely blow up in his face. He is too emotional. Even if I wanted him to do this, he will let his emotions fuck it up. I can never ask him to put a poor girl in that situation just to watch her get hurt. I need to handle this on my own.

I wipe a tear away as more fall. If I would have stayed living in fear, none of this would be happening. I've cried more in front of Archie in the last twenty-four hours than I have from anyone in my chosen family. I drop my hand to my leg. Archie bends over pulling my head into his chest. Holding me just like last night. The way he is reminds me so much of Dillon and William. They have so much love within them that they don't know what to do with it.

Archie seems to be that same way. Everything about him is too familiar. The way he flinches when his phone goes off, how he will run out of the house without saying why. He looks haunted when he comes to school sometimes. There's something in his life that he isn't talking about.

I wipe my eyes sitting back. "I've been told I sound like a Spice Girl."

He smirks and tosses menus at me. I don't know how he can afford to eat out this much and live in this house. Everything is up to date. All of the appliances are up to date, the floors are hardwood. The end tables are glass.

"It'll only come on stronger."

I look around at the high ceiling. The upstairs is surrounded by an indoor balcony. I never looked around much, I just know there is a living room upstairs designated for gaming. "Arch, how can you afford rent in this place?"

"I'm not paying rent, Siren. I own it. My parents bought it out for me."

I really want to pry. His eyes are heavy. He doesn't want to get into it, I need to know. Right now, isn't the right time. "You need to tell me eventually. I will sign a prenup or whatever it's called here. I didn't realise you had money."

He falls back onto his ass hugging his jeans. "If I get you to do that it's just going to look suspicious. If you take half my money, then whatever. I just hope you don't."

Don't worry I won't. I'm hoping I can get you to fall in love with me. "I told the guys I'm marrying you."

He raises his eyebrows.

"Pulling teeth would have been easier. My brothers might or might not kill you."

He smiles smugly for a few seconds before it fades away. "Mum called me a moron. Dad's pissed. Ron's pissed. Marissa's pissed. I think it's safe to say we pissed off the entire world."

This conversation is too easy. There's isn't a funny vibe between us like there should be, there isn't anger or regret. I think he might actually feel at peace with this decision. I thought he was going to back out, not that I wouldn't hold it against him. Instead, he's smiling. He wants his best friend to stay in London.

"So, I guess it's a courthouse wedding?"

"That would be best. We could have an engagement party Saturday, get everyone on board. Convince them you love me."

I nod my head reaching for a smoke. It's not going to be hard to convince them when my hands are tingling, desperate for his touch.

Chapter 7

Archie

I knew this was going to be hard, I need everyone's support on this. Mum and Dad are both being impossible. Marissa won't even look at me and Ron, well he's finally come around. It never took him long. Less than a day. At least everyone agreed to come. It's not really a party, it's just the people who will be vouching for us that we do love each other. Mum, Dad, Marissa, Marissa's mom Melissa, and Ron. It's going to be intimate and extremely intense.

At least with my boss with me all night I can't get pulled away. I think Siren is starting to catch on to me randomly leaving and coming back acting completely different. The weirdest thing is, she knows how to handle me. I don't understand how, she just knows when I need a beer or when I need to sit in silence.

I'm careful about keeping her separate from the Cartel. I think about my words before I choose them. I can't have her finding out about me.

It's only been two days and she's already the best fake fiancé. She's trying harder than any real girlfriend I've seen. It makes me nervous. One day I'm going to wake up forgetting that none of this is real and kiss her when it's just the two of us, or worse, I'll try to sleep with her.

"Arch! Your parents pulled up!" Siren calls out from the entryway of the house. She sounds monotone.

This is going to be a disaster.

Dad storms into the kitchen. He is as tall as I am but thinner. He fights people with mind games and weapons, never physical fights. The look in his eyes, he wants to knock me out. "You're a bloody moron. I never raised you to be this stupid."

I look over this shoulder. My jaw clenches. "No, you just raised me to be in a cartel. Twenty-six days until she's your daughter-in-law."

"Arch, what's going on?" Siren looks terrified. This was a bad idea. She pushes past dad. I put my arms out for her body to pull her in. "Look at me."

I pull my glare from my fathers' sight, to look at her.

"This was a bad idea. It's not too late to call things off. I'm still here for a few more months, we can try the distance thing." Her eyes have a hint of sadness in them.

She's trying to protect me. "If you leave, I'm following you."

Is it stupid to threaten to leave right in front of my boss? Oh, hell yes. I wish she knew that the darkness inside of me has faded. The light in her, even if she doesn't know it's her, has saved me. I'll fight for her, even if it means it's a one-sided fight.

She holds me tighter. I bend down kissing her hair. "I love you."

The first time I've ever said it to a girl and I'm pretending like I only said it to fit the circumstances.

She pulls back, looking up at me. Her eyes twinkle. "I love you too."

This is some kind of cruel joke.

Hayley

"I don't mean to kick you guys out, but Archie needs to be away from his dad." I let out a puff of air.

Screaming and yelling has been the soundtrack for the last hour. I want to know what they are saying, I know it's about me. I don't think they were very close, to begin with, and here I am separating them farther apart. The noise falls quiet, I fly up off my chair and run upstairs.

They are in the living room upstairs. I knock on the wall to make my presence known. "Arch, I told everyone to leave. Come downstairs."

He turns around to leave, his eyes are dark. I've never seen anyone with such black eyes. I may not have seen myself with black eyes, but I felt it. *What the fuck isn't he telling me?* Archie grabs my hand dragging me downstairs. His skin feels ice cold. He leads me into the kitchen away from everyone and plants a kiss on my lips. It's just a small quick peck, but so unnecessary with no one around.

My stomach is starting to twist in knots, it's trying to warn me of something. Everything is all too familiar right now. This is the look of fear on a brainwashed gangster.

"Touch her and I'll blow your fucking head off." Archie's deep voice is in a protective stance. I can't be right about this, I can't be.

The front door slams and Archie's body crashes into mine. He's hugging me so tight that I can feel my ribs wanting to give out. He loses his grip backing away. I grab his shirt by the handful taking a risk. I pull him in closer, giving him a gentle reassuring kiss.

He pushes me off him. "What are you doing?"

My eyes go big, I don't know why I thought that was okay. My eyes are stinging with hot tears. "I just thought." I open the fridge pulling out a beer, shoving it to him before I start crying, again. "You're a good actor, I'm going to bed."

He grabs my wrist. "What do I get out of this arrangement? You get to escape from whatever is it. Don't I get anything? I'm destroying my life for you."

I try to pull my wrist from his grasp. I don't know what his dad said to him, but this person looking back at me is not Archie. It's like his father completely mind fucked him. "You asked me."

I try to plead with him to let go only using my eyes, he has a really tight grip on me. I'm taught how to not squirm, but his strength is almost inhuman.

Something clicks in his eyes and the darkness fades. It's like the realisation hits, he drops my arm letting it fall. "What the fuck am I doing?"

I shake my arm, trying not to cry from the shock and the pain radiating. "What the hell is wrong with you?"

"Siren, my dad he. I'm so sorry."

My hand starts trembling. He's acting more and more like he's brainwashed. I don't understand how. "What's going on?"

"I'll handle it."

"Not very well!" I yell, I'm tired of the half-answers.

Everyone I know has blacked out for a few seconds, including myself. That was how I almost killed Erik and Adam. No matter how many times they explain it to me, I can't remember. I just woke up to Erik stripping off his suit jacket that was united in flames. The searching look on Archie's face looks a hell of a lot like how I felt.

Archie reaches out his hand for me then snaps it back to his body. "Please don't leave. Pour a drink, go have a bath, I bought you bath bombs. Just don't leave me." He raises his shaky hand placing it over his styled hair. "I'm too fucked up for you."

If I'm right on any of this, how the fuck did I fall face-first into another Mafia?

I walk past him, putting my hand on his shoulder. "You need to tell me the truth, Arch. I promise I can handle it."

I love you.

Archie

I haven't gotten a wink of sleep. I've been laying on my couch trying to remember what the hell I said to Hayley. My head hurts, my eyes hurt. The bathroom door opened and closed hours ago. She's probably sleeping. I'm shocked she's still under my roof. How is she still here? I want to forget the look of fear and pain buried deep in her serene eyes. I want to forget the way her hands trembled and the way she yelled. I'm staying up all night in case she leaves, I have no right to stop her. Yet, at the same time, I can't let her go.

"After you are married, I can step down. I get to pass the torch off to you son." My dad's words are replaying in my head. "She's your weakness. If you don't end things, I will end her for you."

I won't let him get that far. This is going to be over before he can retire. I need to protect her, if she walks out on me today, she is saving her own life without knowing it. It's selfish, there's really no words for it. I can't walk away from her. My anger took control of me last night. I've never had problems with anger before and I released it on the wrong person.

The sun is poking through the windows and now its twenty-five days until I marry her, if she still wants to. I need to go lay next to her, maybe if she wakes up, I'll wake up so I can stop her.

I get to the bedroom laying down next to Siren. Even when she is asleep, she is still an enchantress. I don't know how I've lived a life before meeting her. My head hits the pillow, my body is hating me for forcing myself to stay awake. She wakes up extremely early, I don't think her body has adjusted to the time change yet.

It's not even five and she's stirring. She rolls her and her hand lands on my middle. I turn to look at her.

"You finally came to bed." She readjusts the pillow without opening her eyes.

What do I say? Do I apologise for whatever it was I said? How do I even start to explain that she's in danger?

"Archie." Her fingertips touch my cheek before snapping her hand back.

What the hell did I do to her?

I roll over, looking at Hayley. Her facial expression softens. "I'm so sorry."

Her eyes drop down to my lips, which is all I need to get enough courage to kiss her when no one is around. I tangle my hand in her hair pulling her closer to me. Our lips touch and every single part of my body feels like it's shocking me. The blood in my veins is boiling in the best way possible. Her hand runs over the stumble over my jaw line. Even through my exhaustion, the blood shoots down to my dick. I let out a weak groan pulling away from her.

She smiles, laying her head back down. She's bloody smiling because I kissed her. "No one was around, you didn't have to do that."

"I needed to."

"Get some sleep babe, I'll come back from the gym and make breakfast."

We both freeze, realising at the same moment she slipped up.

"Don't kiss me like that. You're screwing with my mind Arch."

I brush her cheek with my hand trying not to smile, "As long as you come back."

"I'll wake you when breakfast is done."

I watch her crawl out of bed and gather her gym clothes. I roll on my back. The girl I love is starting to have feelings for me. How the hell has she not run?

She must be as fucked up as I am.

Chapter 8

Hayley

I've been home for over an hour just long enough to get my coffee made, shower and get my makeup to perfection. It's still chilly outside. The hoodie of my sweater is over my wet hair protecting it somewhat from the winter air. I should be making breakfast for Archie, he just looked so exhausted. I need to let him sleep. I shouldn't even be here. I should be scared of him. I don't want to be scared of him. There's something he isn't telling me, and I care about him too much to run for the hills.

I wiggle around in the patio seats, the house is so nice and yet the patio furniture is so uncomfortable, it's sending shooting pain up my ass to my spine. The backyard is huge, it has so much potential. This yard is big enough for a pool, but a hot tub would be much cheaper. It needs flowerbeds along the fence line and a garden in the back corner.

I'm not even sure if I'm going to live long enough to see it. Me getting married doesn't automatically take me off the Basilisk hit list. I still need to deal with Martin. If I do walk away unharmed, then I'm putting a hot tub out here.

"Siren!" Archie calls out, worry struck in his voice. "Siren!"

I stand from the chair putting my cigarette but in the ashtray. I open the patio door. "I'm right here."

Archie turns around with his hands on his head, running up to me for a hug. "I never smelt food. I thought—" He digs his face in my neck. The fear I thought I managed to get away from lives in Archie.

I rub his back. "What?"

He shakes his head. I'm never going to get an answer out of him.

"I wanted to let you sleep. We can make food now."

He pulls away from me, his eyes don't look as hunted. "No. I got Marissa and Ron on board. We are going to show you London."

"Can we act like friends, or do we have to keep the charade up?"

"Friends. Now go get dressed."

***

This is the day I needed. I never got to experience a new city, I only ever got to sit on the side-lines watching people who dream of a city, experience it. I was on a mission to find a red phone booth, and yes, I got my picture taken with it. It's a foot popping picture and everything. Thankfully, I fixed my wardrobe and actually put care into it. I'm wearing high-rise skinny jeans with a black spaghetti tank top tucked in. I wanted to try to look my best, these are the pictures I'm going to want to have forever.

Archie is already the best fake fiancé ever, I keep putting my jacket on, then taking it off. He doesn't complain when he holds it.

I keep checking my wrist and the scars from the bullets, making sure my foundation is covering everything that needs to be covered.

I heard when people travel they get really happy. I've lived here for a month and I haven't been able to experience any of this. It feels like a vacation that is hopefully never going to end. I'm walking behind Ava, Ron, Marissa and Archie looking around at everything in sight. You don't even need me to talk to know I'm an American. My face is saying it all.

It scares the living shit out of me to see people driving on the wrong side of the road. My heart keeps stopping watching cars turn thinking that they were going to crash into each other.

I look ahead of me, stopping in my tracks to see Archie put his arm over Marissa pulling her in. My chest aches. I never bothered to ask either one of them about their past. I don't even think Marissa likes me much. The way he kissed me this morning, I thought maybe he was starting to feel the same way about me. The way he froze when I accidentally called him babe, his reaction made me freeze. I felt like an idiot. They are both laughing, I don't want to know their history. That's going to be too painful.

I start moving my legs, jogging towards them. They got a head start on me and people got in the middle of us. I reach my arm between him and Ron grabbing my jacket.

My face must be saying how I'm feeling. Archie stops turning around placing his hands on my cheeks. "You alright, Siren?"

"I'm brilliant. I'm just going to run into Starbucks." I place my right hand over his on my cheek. "I can't stop you from being with someone else."

I take a step back pulling my jacket over my shoulders. I walk into Starbucks feeling his hand on my hip pulling me into his body.

He leans down. "You are the one I want to be with."

I pay for my mocha then pull him into the back corner of the building. "Last night you were pissed that you were destroying your life for me Arch. You made it noticeably clear you need something out of this. Maybe I just need to back off and let you date someone you actually love or don't love."

"That's what I said to you?" He pulls his eyebrows together.

I want to start laughing, he blackout, I was right. I look at him with my lips parted. I really hope I'm not right about the rest. "What do you need? You're saving my life. You want to date Marissa again, go for it, and just keep it a secret."

He smirks and I want to backhand him. "We had one date. We've been friends since we were babies."

I grab my mocha walking out of the door.

Archie follows close behind me, "You're cute when you're jealous."

I need to stop doing what I'm doing. He can't know I have real genuine feelings for him. I turn around, looking up at him. The steamed milk in my cup is warming up my hands. Looking into his eyes, running my eyes along his square jaw, the stubble on his face, his full lips that I like to think are screaming for me. "You're my fiancé, who happens to be too attractive for his own good. Of course, I'm jealous. Any wife would be."

He wraps his arm around my shoulder, pulling me in. "I'll pretend like I believe you."

I rest my head on his muscular shoulder. It would be safer if he wasn't involved, I just can't stay away from him. I never wanted to kiss someone so bad in my life. "Thank you for saving me."

"I haven't done anything, not yet." His grip on my shoulder tightens as we walk about to the three impatient faces waiting for us.

Chapter 9

Hayley

I place my palette and paintbrush on the desk looking at my art piece. I never knew what I was drawing until I finished, but this wasn't what I was expecting. It's full of colour. My art has come to life in ways I will never understand. It's surprising too. I painted the empire state building with a colourful sunset behind it. I used reds and pinks for the sky. I thought when I was using red, it was going to represent blood, and it doesn't. I think it represents the life that was stolen from me, the pink is the love that I can't have. The empire state building is a reputation of New York, the city that I learned to hate and love all at the same time.

This is the first time any of my art pieces have seen a touch of colour in them. Maybe that means I'm healing? Or maybe, it means I have accepted my fate. I can be trying to figure out my emotions for hours and be so lost that I can't function. My thoughts won't make sense, it's almost like I don't know who I am until I get a paintbrush in my hand. Then after a few strokes and a few flicks of my wrist, the real me starts to come through. The mist from my eyes is clear and things make sense.

My feeling of homesick started to disappear, then I painted this. Now all I want to do is stand on thirty-Fourth Street and look up. I never got out to see the city, in twenty years I never got to venture off. I regret that now. Being able to tour around London freely was an eye-opener of how much I missed without even noticing.

The second hand is ticking in the clock on the wall above the classroom's board. Everyone is still working. When my mind and hand are connected, I work fast. I can't control it.

Jason walks in with only a few minutes left of class. He runs over to me, putting his hands on my shoulders forcing me to turn. "There are three gorgeous American men outside the cafeteria right now."

My eyes got big, I can feel the tears working their way up. Spencer did mention making a trip, I just never thought Martin would approve it. I really need to be running down there, my legs have turned to stone. My heart is pounding in my chest, I'm scared to see them. I trust them with my life, in fact, I have many times. I know they won't hurt me, that's not what I'm scared of. I'm scared of me missing them all over again.

I wipe my face while fumbling on the table with my other hand for my handbag without looking. "Can you clean up for me?"

"Yes! Go."

I ran out of the classroom bursting through the door. My heartbeat is beating in my ears. Classes have already been dismissed making the hallways packed. I'm trying not to push and shove people out of the way, but three of my people are waiting for me. I don't even care who it is, I will be happy to see any one of them. I finally get through the crowd running down the cement blocks. The courtyard is packed. I let out a sob, tears running down my face.

My vision turns into tunnel vision with William standing directly in front of me. He puts his arms out waiting for a hug. I jump into his arms knowing he will catch me. I wrap my legs around his waist burying my face into his neck. My hair is wrapping around his five o'clock shadow stubble. I let out a sob, feeling a tiny bit of myself being put back together.

He rubs my back, his chest vibrating. "We only have until tomorrow morning."

He moves his hands down my hips pulling me off of him. My feet hit the cement. My arm is pulled into another body. I know it's Josh, he is the only one that is the same height as me. He is holding me tighter than I ever thought was possible. It doesn't matter that we are only half-siblings, we grew up together. We are best friends.

His chest gives off a shaky breath. A tear rolls down my face landing on his shoulder. I think a part of us all thought we were never going to see each other again.

Josh pushes me away from him. "You got ugly."

I roll my eyes, wiping my face. Because of me, Josh and Spencer started their own nonbiological brotherhood relationship. They are both very immature with each other and sometimes I'm pulled in by my hair.

I swat his arm looking up at Spencer. "You guys both got fat."

I use all the strength I have left to hug Spencer, he holds me tightly in return.

I take a step back, looking around. There are only a few people left in the courtyard. I'm speechless, I don't know why they are here. The only reason why they would be here is if it's work-related.

Suddenly, Archie's cologne is circulating around me, he puts his hands on my hips from behind. I let myself fall in his embrace. He brushes his lips against my cheek, "Everyone kept asking me why my fiancé is running into someone's arms."

I turn around reaching up, putting my elbows on his shoulder, holding my hands behind his head. "Do you mind if they crash at your place tonight?"

"Siren, it's not just my house anymore. Go have fun. I love you."

I bring my lips up to his kissing him, he only said it for the act. I am disappointed, but I can't force him to have feelings for me. "I love you, Arch."

I drop my hands running them down his chest gazing into his eyes. My hand meets his, we both back away, turn around and our hands separate from the space we are creating between each other.

Spencer and Josh are both glaring down at Archie.

William shakes his head. "If you would have just told us you guys loved each other, we wouldn't be so pissed about you marrying him."

I push Spencer's and Josh's shoulders backwards to break their glares. "We don't, it was an act for everyone around."

Josh laughs once loudly. "No one's around."

Spencer pulls me to his side. "Joshua, our little sister is in love."

***

Sitting in Archie's living room with three of my favourite people doesn't feel real. I still keep catching myself wishing Archie was here too so he can learn to love them like I do. I never get to see the Basilisks in regular jeans and sweaters. It's so refreshing knowing they have a break, even if it's just for a day. We are all beating around the bush on why they are here. No one wants to say those words. I'm waiting for William to just tell me. One of the best things about him is that he will be blunt with you. I don't know if that's because he's a Taylor and growing up with his dad informing him of the Boss bloodline at a young age, or if he picked it up along the way.

Even William is avoiding the tense air. I'm starting to think I'm going to have to bring it up. I don't know if I can. I don't want to destroy our time.

I breathe through my lips making them vibrate. "Why are you guys here?"

William sets his drink down and slouches back into the couch. "Martin sent us to track you down and bring you back. We never found you though."

"We never found you, but Martin isn't just going to quit. He is going to send people here if he finds out where you are." Josh pours my cup full. "You need to watch your back."

Do I tell them what I think is going on with Archie or will that cause too much stress on them on top of what I already started? I place my elbows on my knees holding my head at my hairline with my fingers. Martin isn't going to be able to find me. I'm going to go back to New York, and he is going to be able to notice hints of my British accent coming through, then he will know where I've been hiding. By then I'll be married, and I'm hoping that will be just enough for him to want to spare my life.

I reach for my cup on the end table, chugging it back. Trying to prepare myself to say words that I'm not even sure to be true out loud. "I think Archie is involved with something. He got in a fight with his dad and told him he was going to blow his head off if he touched me. I'm not sure if he remembers it. That's too similar to our father's relationships. He has our sadness and fear in his eyes. I think he was shot."

Spencer puts his tongue in his tooth. "He might just have shitty luck." He shrugs. "If it is true, at least you're safe."

Josh smacks Spencer. "Dude, no! If he is and he finds out she's a Basilisks isn't that fuck, I don't know? Double-crossing spy shit?"

I've been so worried about trying to figure out the truth about Archie, it never crossed my mind how bad it was going to look on his end. The colour has washed out of my face, my makeup is gone only making me look paler. How is this my life three thousand miles away? How did I bring all my garbage with me to another continent?

I never even heard the door open and close. Archie is standing in front of me looking as worried as I feel. "Siren you alright?"

That seems to be the only thing he ever asks me. I need to work on hiding my emotions.

I give a weak smile. "I'm just panicking about the flight at Easter. I hate flying."

Archie is looking at me like I'm stupid. He saw right through that lie. "If you are fake marrying me to get away, why are you going back?"

"Unfinished business."

"Half answers? Seriously Hayley? That's all I get?"

"You better start giving me full answers then."

We are both being unfair to each other. We are both clearly hiding something from one another. I don't know about him, but I'm trying to protect him from my truth. I'm not going to cave and tell him. The truth is too much for anyone to process. I can tell William, Spencer and Josh are all looking uncomfortable putting their own pieces of our screwed-up puzzle together. This is our first fight and of course, there are witnesses.

I wish I could read his mind. I need to know what is going on in there. As scary as his thoughts might be, I need to know. I thought him calling me Siren was weird at first, now I just feel uncomfortable when he says my name. It's like he's furious at me without actually saying that he's mad.

Archie groans. "Siren, some things are just better not said. If you can't understand it fine, dig. Just don't be pissed at me when you know the truth." He scrubs his face with his hands. "I know you have an ex in New York if you see him. Please don't tell me about it. I just don't want to bloody know."

He walks away back out the front door. His words are lingering over me. I never thought there was any chance that he would be feeling the same way about me, that possibility just blew a door wide open. I want to dig into his life, it just doesn't feel right. If he isn't going to tell me, do I risk breaking his trust, and anything he might be feeling might start to decay around me before I'm certain of how he's actually feeling?

"What do I do?" I hold my head in my hands, tears are burning in my eyes once again.

"Nothing," William said simply. "You marry him, and you stay the hell away from Liam."

Archie

Ron tosses me his pack of Marlboros, I pinch the brown filter putting the fag between my lips. The shocked look on Siren's face before I walked out, how bloody oblivious can she be? I can't think about this, I wish I wasn't. She has consumed every inch of my mind since the first time I ever laid my eyes on her. I have other things I need to focus on at this very moment. For once I need to pull my mind away from her. It seems impossible.

The semi pulls up with cars pilled on. Every time we have a delivery from Columbia, we need to switch our locations. We never hit the same spot within a six-month period and never in the same order. I'm not sure how, but so far, it's been working.

Ever since the other night, my dad hasn't even acknowledged me. Not that I'm complaining. Being away from him is giving me time to try to come up with a game plan. Even though nothing is coming to my mind. Absolutely nothing.

I walk to the first car that's been unloaded, Ron takes the second car. I rip up a piece in the corner by the driver's side floor. The floors are fake, lined with drugs. I walk over to the passenger seat checking the floors on this side and the same thing. I move the zipper only a tiny bit of the way and the seat is full. I do the exact same thing to the back seat, pop open the trunk checking under the boards.

I let out a puff of air, what kind of shitty person brings in this many drugs. There are five other cars exactly the same.

The cars aren't fancy, they are just basic hatchbacks in basic colours. I don't know if smuggling drugs in cheaper vehicles is easier. To me, it would raise more red flags. I'm just one person though. Whatever my Dad has figured out, it's been working for him.

As soon as one of us checks and okay the vehicles they get delivered to the Baker Cartel after being transported three thousand miles.

Ron walks past me walking back to his car. "Why is Alfie cutting back on the amount?"

I squint my eyes looking into the sun. He isn't wrong, this is the first delivery we have had in weeks. "It must have to do with Jeremy's tips."

Ron looks up at me over the car hood. "We're fucked."

I press my lips together nodding.

I open the door to the house listening to the squeal of Ron's tires against the pavement. The instant I turn the door handle a haze of smoke comes wafting towards me on the front porch. *How the hell can four people create this much smoke?*

I shut the door and suddenly Siren has me wrapped up in her warm embrace. "I'm so sorry. I won't dig."

I wrap my arms around her holding her. I almost feel relief that she isn't going to be snooping. I'm also panicking about her being in danger when I'm away from her. I tighten my grip resting my chin on her hair. I've been holding her for way too long, I'm aware of that. She hasn't let go. I'm holding onto the hope that maybe she isn't as oblivious as I thought.

I loosen my arms letting her step away from me.

Siren points to a memory foam pad. "Marissa dropped that off, why?"

"It's for whoever is stuck on the spare bed." I shrug. "Now you don't have to sleep in the same bed with me if you don't want to. Let you have space from me for once."

She takes a step back studying me like I'm studying her. Her smile faded the more I talked, until she's standing in front of me with her lips in a hard line. I close my eyes, almost preparing us for another argument. I don't know what I said wrong. Whatever it was, it's written all over her face.

She scrunches her nose. "Your bed's so comfy though." She pauses only for a second. "Do I wake you up at night?"

I wasn't sure if she knew she had nightmares. I wanted to ask her. I never knew how to bring it up. "Not for a few days."

"Get in here, I want to meet your boyfriend." Someone from the living room called out.

Every time Siren blushes it's like she challenges me. She tries to show me that she isn't flattered. Only this time, she turns her head away from me. Like she's hiding from me.

I have a smug smile on my face, and I don't care. I am winning Siren over, whether she likes it or not. I intertwine my fingers with her feeling numbness shoot up my arm. I still don't understand how she has come into my life flipping everything upside down without even trying.

Feeling like she was immune to my charm and good looks makes a lot more sense after today. Hearing comments from Marissa and Ava about the three men sitting in my living room glaring at me, makes a lot more sense. She is immune to it all. She was raised with guys exactly like me. Well, not exactly like me. Obviously with some huge differences.

Very huge differences.

I sit down, Siren brings me a cup half full of amber liquid. I look up at her to see her smirking. She walks away light-footed.

Now that I have a girl in my life, and in my house, I need her to use her feminine touch and decorate this place. My walls are bare, I have a big screen TV hanging on the wall. Other than my glass coffee tables, leather couch, loveseat and matching chair, it's empty. I live in an oversized bachelor pad.

My eyes bounce between the four of them casually sipping their Whiskey. I feel like an armature, I can't even handle the smell. I hold the cup, their eyes are plastered onto me. I have never been judged as hard as I am at this very moment. I don't know what to do, I've dated before, but I've never felt like *this* before. We aren't together, but I can't act like someone who doesn't have feelings for her. I also can't act like someone who has feelings for her.

I'm overthinking this. I feel like a woman. Is this why they are always so bitchy?

Siren laughs nervously. She pauses, then continues to laugh. "He's not going to break."

I look up at her and she smiles, mouthing, *"Sorry."*

"I'm Josh, that's Spencer and that's William." Josh points as he goes.

Josh and Spencer look nothing alike. They both kind of look like Siren. They share a few of the same features. Josh and Hayley have the same downward turned eye shape and they are almost the exact same height. While Spencer and Hayley have the same face structure.

Being able to place three faces with names feels a hell of a lot better.

Hayley stands up walking to the counter. "I almost forgot, we got mail today."

She turns around and her hand is shaking. I set my undrunk whiskey on the table flying up from the couch. I don't even need to see the return address or the official government stamp to see what it is. I put my hand out, she drops them letting out a shaky breath.

I open it reading the words faster than my brain can comprehend what it says. "Everything went through."

Bloody hell.

I have no idea how any of this worked. It must be a fault in the system, I'm not going to say anything. I can't lose her.

The guys all let out a puff of air from their lungs that they were holding. I don't know what she is running from, all I know is that the relief they are feeling is making me feel it too. Hayley is looking at me with tears in her eyes. She's frozen.

"Siren—"

She puts her hand in front of me with her palm facing me. She lets out a small giggle cutting me off. "Don't ask me if I'm alright."

"If you don't want to do this—"

Siren cuts me off, again. "No, we're doing this."

"Good. Since this is actually happening can I come to New York with you?"

She stares at me blank-faced.

I feel pretty damn humiliated right now. It's a wedding on paper, not a real wedding. I asked her not to tell me about her ex so I'm probably looking pretty pathetic right about now.

"Right, fake wedding. I'm going to bed. You know where the spare pillow and blankets are."

I turn away not glancing at the guys sitting on the couch. I don't look back to Siren. It felt like we were starting to move forward, then suddenly we come to an abrupt stop. I'm trying to not show my annoyance in my footsteps walking up the stairs, it's almost impossible to try to hide how I am feeling. It may be a fake wedding but that doesn't change the fact she is still my best friend and I want to meet everyone else in her life.

I get to the doorway, it's useless to even try and make out what they are saying. They are speaking in such hush tones. My body freezes at the sound of Siren letting out a sob. I turn around running down the stairs. I don't care how moody I look today, she makes all logic and sense of direction go up in smoke.

She is leaning against Josh on the couch wiping her face. He leans up, making her sit up. She almost looks shocked that I ran back down here for her.

I lean over pulling her into me. I kiss her forehead, brushing my lips against her skin. "Come to bed." I stand up reaching my hand out for her to grab it, not taking my eyes off her. "Blankets are in the closet of the bedrooms. They are upstairs with the door open. The pads for the beds are by the front door in boxes. Eat whatever you find."

Siren stands squeezing Williams's shoulder. He looks up at me making eye contact nodding once. The TV is already on, I feel like I should have done more. Siren is the only thing on my mind and right now, I could care less if they like me or not.

She shouldn't be this upset by not wanting me to go to New York with her, she was fine until I asked her. I need to know what she is hiding.

She opens our bedroom door and slides in grabbing her clothes. Then walks back out again not saying a single word to me, or even looking in my direction. I take my shirt off, along with my pants tossing a random pair of pyjama pants on and slide into my bed on the bed by the wall.

Siren comes back in, I'm half-surprised she even came to bed with me. She lays down on her side facing away from me. I'm on my back staring into the darkness of my room. I want to cuddle her, or even just touch her. I don't know what set her off. I don't know if it was me, or her getting to be with her ex again, maybe she's just homesick. I just want to know, so I know if I'm allowed to touch her or not.

"I can't get anything right with you today." The words that are going to get me in the most trouble slipped out of my mouth.

She pulls up the blanket. I can't see her, I'd imagine she is covering half her face.

"If you didn't want me to go so you could be with him, just tell me. I don't know how far you want this marriage thing to go."

"Arch." She rolls over, sliding her hand over the comforter until she meets my arm. "I don't want to be with Liam."

"Can you tell me what it is? It would be nice not to feel like I'm not walking on the gates of hell."

"Dramatic much?" Hayley rolls back over. "Can you cuddle me? I just want to be held."

Music to my ears. I roll over facing her, pulling her body into mine. She grabs a hold of her hair placing it under her head on the pillow. I burry my face into her neck smelling her grapefruit lotion. I kiss her neck listening to a singsong hum leave her throat.

This is as close to heaven as I'm ever going to get.

Chapter 10

Hayley

I have felt way too many waves of emotions and I hate it. I hate every bit of it. My family was only here for a few hours and it was more of a tease than anything. I trusted them not to kidnap me and bring me back to New York. I just didn't realise how hard I was going to have to stop myself from buying a ticket and going with them. They came and I started to feel homesick again. The dull ache in my chest started, my eyes began to burn. I'm seriously sick and tired of crying. I don't cry. Now suddenly it's all I do. All of my pint up hidden stress from being a Basilisk under Martin's brainwashing control is starting to be set free since I freed myself.

Archie is asking me to come to New York with him, I would want nothing more. I just don't know how to tell him he might be getting on a plane to London alone. I don't remember why I am even going back. If I was smart, I would stay away from Martin. If I show my face, he is going to take the chance and kill me right there. How am I supposed to tell Archie not to come with me?

Spencer told me to tell Archie. In his experience, it worked out for him. Cameron found out about the Basilisks the day they officially met. I never let him finish, I had never seen someone so in love. He hides her away from everyone who doesn't live with him to keep her safe. We all know what she looks like from school, but we never met her. His story is encouraging me, if he is able to keep her safe, I can keep Archie safe halfway across the world.

Josh told me to figure out what's going on in his life first then decide if it would be too dangerous.

William told me to just sleep with him.

It's a good thing I wasn't expecting William to be of any help because he wasn't. Him telling me to stay away from Liam is easy. It sounds bad, I just know I'm going to see him and get lost in his hypnotising grey eyes. He's hands down the sexiest person ever, it's easy to be hypnotised by him.

I look in the mirror, I have nowhere to go today but my old habits of always looking nice are staying with me. My long hair is in a backcombed ponytail. My makeup is in neutral colours like always and my thick-framed cat-eyed dark blue glasses are hugging the bridge of my nose. I step out of the bathroom and Archie walks down the hall, he's been MIA the past few days. It's only been making my theory about him a lot more believable.

"You're beautiful," Archie says, sounding dumbfounded.

I look away feeling my cheeks burn. I hate what he does to me, but I love it all at the same time.

"It's not for a few weeks yet. Marissa booked you and Ava an appointment to do your hair and nails before the ball."

I scrunch my nose looking at his body, I want to jump on him so bad. "She doesn't have to pretend to like me."

My eyes move up to his, he is undressing me with his eyes. He isn't being discreet about it. He's slowly scanning my arms, shoulders, neck, and the seam of my V-neck long sleeve shirt. Being under his fixated gaze feels nothing but perfect. My legs can hardly support my body. Would giving into this tension screw things up if I sleep with him, or will everything fall into place?

He clears his throat. His eyes making their way up to mine. They are glossed with lust and desire.

I've only ever slept with one person before and I was dating him. I can't give in, it is going to mess everything up for me. It would only screw with my mind. I already want to scream at him and tell him I'm in love with him. Sex would just amplify everything I'm already feeling.

Screw it. I take a step forward. Archie does the same. His hands almost land on my hips as the doorbell rings.

"That is probably a good thing," Archie mumbles so slowly I almost can't make out what he said.

I need to rethink going back to New York, I need to stay here with him. If there is any chance, he was thinking the same thing I was, I need to let this play out in the safety of my fiancé's arms.

"Siren, I need to talk to you. I just want you to know what you are getting yourself into with me." Archie walks away looking white as Casper.

Before I can even organise my thoughts, the door opens, and Archie shields my body with his slamming me into the wall behind me. My shoulders hit it hard, almost hard enough to put a dent in the wall. I don't think Archie understands how strong he really is.

What the fuck is happening? His eyes look black like hell is breaking loose.

"You really suck at answering your door," Marissa calls from downstairs.

His hands hit the wall behind me. He looks down at me and kisses my forehead. "Don't just walk in."

Neither of us is fighting to move away from the graze of our eyes. I can see the aqua coming back into his dark eyes. I'm only inches away from his face, the lust I feel towards him is still in my eyes. I'm fighting my arm not to reach up and pull his neck down for our lips to finally meet again.

"Don't give me a key then." Marissa's feet paddle against the floorboard on the stairs. "Oh, sorry."

My chest is beating out of my body. I just need Archie to say it. He tenses when his phone goes off, the darkness and fear that appear in his eyes all too often, the way he blacked out, the way he shields me. Minus him dressing up every day, he's living the life I ran away from. He pushes himself off the wall and steps back, his breathing is starting to lighten up. I want to rub my shoulders to loosen up the pain, I just don't want him to feel bad about his reflection in protecting me.

Marissa's eyes are bouncing back between the both of us. Her hair is getting longer, and her dark roots are showing. Her style is a little bit flashier than mine, she adds belts. Other than that she is pretty plain like I am. I look to the corner of my eye half dreading to see Archie's gaze on her, instead, his eyes are locked on me. I feel like I'm melting into the ground. The way he looks at me is indescribable. The twinkle in his eyes is almost blinding. He doesn't look like that towards anyone else.

I don't know what it feels like to be loved by anyone other than Liam, but I'd imagine it feels something close to this.

I reach out my hand to graze the skin on his arm with my fingertips. "When you want to talk let me know. I'll let you guys do your thing."

"I came for you mate." Marissa's eyes focus on me rather than me and Archie. "I need new clothes. I don't want to go alone."

I nod my head trying not to look too surprised. "Let's go."

***

A Saturday in a mall in the city, that's something I've always tried to avoid. I'm used to being around a lot of random people outside on the sidewalks. Being inside with the same amount of people plus more makes me feel something close to claustrophobic.

Marissa is the easiest person to go shopping with, she likes something, tries it on then buys it. There's no questioning, or me trying to talk her into something. It's great, being friends with girls isn't something I'm used to.

There were only ever two in my life and one of them kind of left me when I broke up with Liam for the final time. Violet is his cousin, it just made sense. April his sister has been dating Josh off and on as I have with Liam. She has a temper on her and most of the time it's like I add gasoline onto her flame. Dillon and William never got the chance to leave me. They are way too close to me, plus it would make no sense when Liam still hung around me.

It never really made sense for Violet or April to walk away either. I'm not complaining though, girls cause headaches and unnecessary drama. Especially those two. Violet went insane when I hurt Liam swearing up and down to watch his back for the next girl he dates. April being mad at me is understandable. Liam resorted to sleeping with all her

90

friends and that caused a lot of tension between the two, even more than there already was.

I'm piling shirts, shorts, dresses and skirts on my arm off the clothing racks. I take a deep breath getting lost in my thoughts. "Do you think Arch would mind if I buy some art or something to make it look like we actually live there?"

Marissa laughs. "I was wondering how long it would take you to decide it needed some love."

"Would it be me overstepping?"

Marissa goes quiet, shutting down the entire idea. I need to know why she doesn't like me, or why she acts like she doesn't like me. It probably has to do with the fact we are getting married and everything's a huge sham, there has to be more to it. Dealing with overprotective people isn't anything new to me, I'm just not used to dealing with overprotective people when they aren't on my side.

I take my stack of clothes to the register, preparing myself. "Why did you even get me to come?"

She sighs. "I wanted to see if you could trick me like you did him."

"What the hell are you talking about?" I turn around facing her in the line. "I'm not trying to trick him, I haven't done anything to mislead him."

"I'm not talking about misleading him. I'm talking about his money."

I shake my head. If she could see the zeros in my bank account from all my blood money for the last four years, we would not be having this discussion. "I didn't even know he has money. His parents bought the house."

Marissa closes her eyes tightly. Without knowing it she just made my theory more set in stone. A university student who owns his own house that's as big as the one he has. Blood money.

I turn back around as the cashier calls out next. I watch her scan and fold the clothes then stuff them into the oversized brown paper bag. Even with the amount I bought it is a fraction of what two outfits would have cost me in New York. Not having a wardrobe is a wonderful feeling. I may have a lot of money in my account, but it doesn't mean I want to look like I do. I punch the pin for my debit in the pin pad, take the receipt and walk out of the store not waiting for Marissa.

I get where she is coming from, I do. I just hate being accused of something when I don't even know the full story.

Before I walked into the clothing store, I noticed an art store across the hall, that's what triggered my thoughts. The store is huge with paintings I recognise from famous artists and other artists that are not quite famous but working their way up. It is a dream of mine to have copies sold in a store like this, it always seemed so far-fetched. Now, if I survive, the odds are going to be more in my favour.

I don't care if Marissa says I'm overstepping. I probably am. That's not her decision to make. If Archie feels that way, he can put it out on the curb with the garbage on Monday or return it.

Walking around I see art that people travelling would buy. I live in London, it would look strange to have a piece in the living room with Big Ben, or a red phone booth on the wall. It would be like going to someone's house in New York and seeing a big statue of liberty on the wall.

There's a lot of abstract, I just don't think Arch would appreciate it. I want something that he will appreciate, less likely for him to throw it to the curb. If he hasn't decorated his house at all since he bought the house, he might not take me too lightly on buying anything for it.

One wall is lined up with forests, beaches, oceans and mountains. The wall across from it has wildlife, mostly wolves, bears, elephants, tigers. I want to throw my hands in the air, I'm about to give up. I don't know enough about him to try and put something in his living room.

"Buy something you want. Don't worry about what Archie is going to think of it." Marissa is dragging her feet towards me. "I'm sorry. I figured he told you he bought his house. I thought you would have clued in this is his family money when his mom throws balls."

If only she knew he already turned down me asking if he wanted a prenup to save his family's money.

I ignore her half-apology and continue to look around. A very large piece catches the corner of my eye. If I am buying something, I want it to be this. His place is all dull colours, this will pop out on the wall. The canvas is white, it looks like there is a city drawn out in thin black ink. The lines are covered in splotches of colour ranging from yellow, orange, blue, purple, pink and red. It's one of those pieces where you look at it and everyone would see something different. For me, it's diversity living as one.

The worker comes up behind me. "We deliver."

I smile. "Good, it's way too big."

Chapter 11

Archie

I open the door to see a man in his fifties standing in front of me. He is half my size in height and muscle. He doesn't pull his eyes from the clipboard in his hands, there is a white van outside the house with the word's *masterpiece delivery.*

"Hayley Cohen?"

I make a straight line with my lips. *Yes, mate I'm Hayley.* "She isn't home."

"I just need you to sign this for pick up."

He hands me the clipboard and another man is carrying the awkward sized parcel to the door. I sign handing it back, he rips off a copy for me. *What on earth is six feet tall and three feet wide?* I'm not stupid, I know it's a painting. I grab the painting from the other man and awkwardly shuffle into the house shutting the door behind me.

I want to open it.

Why isn't she home yet? My stomach does a flip in my stomach. Dad is still threatening her life, the art got delivered before she got here. I pull out my phone unlocking it as fast as my fingers will let me.

I pull out her contact trying not to jump to the conclusion that she's dead somewhere.

"Arch, you miss me or something?" I hear a smile in her voice, and my heart starts to go back to its regular rhythm.

"Where are you?"

It sounds like she is sucking in the air. "I don't know. I needed a drink after being with Marissa. Your co-worker Jack is here. Archie…I didn't even know you had a job."

"Tell him I say to drive you home. That's what I wanted to talk to you about."

I hear him agree, in the distance. "See you soon."

I hang up the phone before the words I love you slip off my tongue. If I trust Siren with anyone other than Ron, it is Jack. We grew up together but we weren't really close. Our dad's had a falling out when he became boss. It wasn't until university that we got closer. Then one day he couldn't handle the Cartel and school, so he dropped out. Not like I can blame him. The cartel steals your soul right out of your body. I've confined in him, he's been trying to help me come up with a plan to destroy the Baker Cartel. Both of us keep coming up blank. Either way, how this plays out, the cops are going to have our arses.

Telling Siren everything is going to be bad. I'm going to lose her before I even finish talking. Everything that is unfolding for us is going to be slammed shut. I know she knows that there is something here between us, she might not think it's a big thing. She doesn't feel it as intense as I do, it doesn't matter, after tonight I'm going to be alone. My best friend, my future wife, everything I love is going to walk away from me.

The room is silent and hazy from my fagging. I can't remember the last time I was this stressed out. I want to shoot something, maybe with the pull of the trigger, all of this will leave my body.

The door opens and I fly up from the couch meeting Siren at the door.

She looks at me staring at my toes, all the way up to my eyes. "If you don't like it just tell me."

She takes a step to the side, ripping open the white protective cover. It is six feet tall of coloured splatter. Artists are weird.

"What do you think?" She looks up at me with big eyes.

I blink slowly.

"I knew you'd hate it. I can get them to come and pick it up."

I can hear how hurt she is. I want to understand this side of her. I grab her forearm lightly. "Explain it."

She laughs. "You can't explain art. Just look at it, really look at it."

I'm looking at it and all I see is rainbow splatter. I tip my head to the right and left, hoping that maybe something will stand out. I can feel her gorgeous sparkling serene eyes on me. I shake my head, I don't know what I'm looking for.

She points to an almost invisible black line behind the colours. "That looks like a building."

I cross my arms examining it. "No, it doesn't. You know that thing on pirate ships they would stand on to look into the distance? That's what it looks like." I point. "That's the ship." I frown, pulling my arm back. "It's the tears of people lost at seas. You're dark Siren. Maybe I picked the right name for you after all."

I can see her face become long in the corner of my eye and her mouth drops. "It's diversity in a city!"

I face her with my arms still crossed and my eyebrows raised.

She smirks. "This is why I love art, no one sees the same thing as someone else. Everyone's viewpoints are different."

I wish Siren could see herself in my eyes at this very moment. The way she is holding herself, the twinkling in her eyes. The smile that is spread across her face. There is no doubt in my mind that there has never been a more beautiful soul to walk this earth. She has so much wisdom in her in such a short amount of time on this earth. I love her more than I ever thought loving someone was possible and now I need to pull her away from me. There's no way she is going to stay with me after this. I need to tell her now before it's too late.

I reach down for her hand intertwining my fingers with hers. If she is going to walk away, I may as well have a few less regrets on my mind. "Come sit down. We can hang it after we talk."

She squeezes my hand, almost like she's trying to reassure me. Her other hand is brushing my arm.

Hayley

It feels like I'm going to pass out. I lean into my legs, my elbows supporting my body. I thought it was my mind playing tricks on me, I thought I was overreacting to everything. How the hell was I born into the Basilisks only to run away and now be in danger because of the Baker Cartel? Archie never told me why I'm in danger, honestly, I couldn't be more thankful. I don't think I would be able to stomach it.

I know it's hypocritical for me to judge him. Martin smuggles in weapons like they are boxes of puppies. Drugs are an entirely new level. Maybe it's not, chances are it's just the shock that's making me think this. Like me he was born into this life, neither of us had a chance.

I hold my head fighting down the words *I'm a Basilisk.* He doesn't need to know, hopefully, he will never find out. How am I supposed to be okay with this? I ran and now I'm on a hit list, only to be a future Cartel wife. Life isn't supposed to be like this.

"Siren, say something please." Archie's voice is muffled by his hand.

"What do you want for dinner?" I ask without looking in his direction.

He laughs in disbelief. Not from humour, there isn't a single funny thing that he just told me. The only comforting thing about this, he's killed a quarter of the men I have. His Dad doesn't send out hits like it's the only option, he doesn't act out hits from other people and pocket the money. Alfie wants me dead. I want him dead even more.

"I'm an emotional eater. I also want a drink. Let's go out." I stand reaching for his hand.

Archie doesn't carry a gun on time at all times. The guys have a permanent gun holster under the suits, mine was always safely secured in my purse. His last name is different from his dad's to keep the focus off him. My head is spinning, our lives are so much alike, but different all at the same time.

He stands and it's like an invisible force field dragging me into his arms. I'm a bad guy, he's a bad guy. We don't deserve any type of happiness. Just like me, he is living in fear. Just like me, he understands what it truly feels like to be living in hell. He just may never know the life I'm hiding from him. I can't protect him as much as I want to, but I sure as hell will protect him from the Basilisks.

He squeezes me between his arms placing his face in my neck. "You don't have to stay Hayley. Whatever it is you're hiding from, you're going to be safer there."

"Do you want me to go?" I push out the question, bracing myself for the dreaded truth.

Archie shakes his head.

"Let's go to the bar, eat, drink, come home and pass out. I'm not going anywhere."

He grabs onto me holding me tighter than ever before. It's like his life is depending on me. I know what it's like to find freedom in someone, I just didn't realise he found it in me.

We get to the bar and Archie has his arm around me walking in. It's a Saturday night and with what I'd assume it's like clockwork, it's packed with university students. Not that I would know, I've never been here on a Saturday night. The first table I spot has both Ava and Marissa at it. I feel my body cringe starting at my toes all the way up to my neck.

I step out from under Archie's arm running to Jason who's walking over to the bar. I latch onto his arm. "I'm surprised to see one of my classmates here, you guys are all so weird."

Jason grins. "Coming from the one who calls chips fries."

"Chips are a deep-fried heaven and fries are potatoes." I squint my eyes at my own words hoping he's too drunk to notice my stupidity.

I lean against the bar ordering my single malt Irish neat whiskey. I really do have the drinking habits of a forty-year-old man, I could care less. I put the glass to my lips slowly sipping on it.

"If I was straight, I would say that's pretty hot." Jason pushes himself straight up from leaning on the bar next to me.

Archie stands behind me kissing my cheek. I wish every second of every single day could feel like this. "If you were straight I'd have to knock you out, mate."

Jason waves him off.

"I'm going to go sit with Marissa and order. Are you going to come?"

His question is lingering in the air. It's not a simple are you going to come to eat, it's so much more than that. It's do you still want to be seen with me?

I turn around searching for his lips. He leans over almost as urgently as I feel. I pull away, my mind is cursing me. "I don't think I should. It's not because of you Arch."

He tightens the arm that is wrapped around my lower back. "Why did you need a drink so bad after shopping with her? What happened?"

I'm running a pro and con list in my mind about telling him. If I don't tell him he's only going to find out, then be annoyed I kept it from him. I keep my tone low enough that the words that are meant for him will only be heard by him. "I had no idea you owned your house. Not until Marissa accused me of marrying you for your money."

He flexes his jaw.

"It's not a big deal. She's watching out for you. I didn't know you had money." Trying to make myself clear right now is useless, of course, I had no idea.

"It's not okay."

He moves his hand from my lower back down to my hand leading me to their table. Ava has cleared for now and Ron has taken the spot next to Marissa.

I can feel by how tight Archie is holding my hand that he is furious. "What the hell Marissa?" He doesn't sound as mad as I thought he was. He sounds mentally exhausted.

"Archie…" She starts talking and stops mid-sentence.

"Don't bother talking to me until you can accept Siren. I don't want to deal with you being jealous."

Marissa drops her jaw.

"No. Not over me." I force my hand from Archie's placing it on my backcombed hair. "I'm going to go home and go to bed. You can stay and figure whatever the hell this is. Just remember you don't actually love me." My voice is cheerful, other than the haunting hurt look in my eyes, you would never be able to guess the tugging sensation that my heart is feeling in this very second.

Archie

"Hayley." Before she even gave me a chance to fight for her to stay, she is walking out of the building.

Ron pats the table before getting up to leave. I'm so tired of this fight with Marissa. I gave her a change, it wasn't there. She told me nothing was there for me either, so why the hell is she still trying?

I collapse in the booth. My night is destroyed. Siren almost took the breaking news about me too well. Making it easier on me, but almost scarier at the same time.

I drop my hands on the table ready to start demanding answers. "What is your deal?"

"You deserve to be with someone who wants to be with you, not citizenship."

"It's never been you. Either you can get over it, befriend my wife or walk away."

Marissa laughs once high pitch, "You say wife like it actually means something to you. You aren't even married yet and you can't even call your rubbish."

"Arch, you have my phone." Siren touches my arm, sending a cooling sensation rushing up my body.

I cover her hand with mine. "I'm coming home with you."

I turn around to face Marissa instantly regretting the words. "You're my best friend, but so is she. I'm not going to stand here while you put ideas in her or my head. You don't know the full story. I just want my friend back."

I walk away with Hayley's hand still in mine. She is practically running trying to keep up with my fast pace walking. Too much has happened today, I just want to lay down in bed and pretend like everything in my life is perfect. I want to understand how she took the news so well. Why she is holding my hand right now is a mystery. It was selfish of me to ask her to stay, I should have told her to run as fast as she could in the other direction. I couldn't even bring myself to speak.

We get in a cab, not driving here was useless. Neither of us even finished a full drink. She's on the other side of the backseat, she's only an arms distance from me. Despite that, she feels like she's thousands of miles away. I need to man up and pour my feelings onto her. Our wedding is in two weeks. She'll be mine forever. It still isn't enough.

I need to get laid.

Having her in the same bed as me is just tempting me to slip my hand under her pyjamas or surprise her with a kiss, and not pull away just to see where she will take it. Even if I didn't feel this way about her, I would still be screwed, no self-respecting woman is going to sleep with an engaged man.

Two months ago, I never had this problem, I could call a girl up and they were at my house in a flash. Then this enchantress from America just shows up one day and suddenly I can't even think about getting it up for anyone else.

I pass the cab driver money, not fully paying attention to the bills knowing he is getting a bloody big tip. Neither of us said a word to each other on the way home. I know her, and with how close she is with her friends in New York, she is going to try to fight for me and Marissa to be friends.

I unlock the door, turning the light on. Siren is already halfway up the stairs. I close my eyes, taking a deep breath. It's almost like she is trying to be easy to read, even though it's impossible all at the same time. Why not make an already exhausting day more exhausting, let's just toss an argument in there too?

I walk up the stairs. Women suck. I also need them, so I'm stuck in a hard place. The pipes for the shower are creaking. I quickly change before falling onto the black comforter shirtless.

"Arch. Can you please bring me clothes?" Siren calls from the bathroom.

I stand up collecting whatever I see first, the door is opened a crack with her arm sticking out of it. I pass them to her not saying a word, not knowing what I can say. I wish I could be a mind reader. Get me a few steps ahead at least.

I fall back on the bed waiting for her long legs to carry herself in the room. She doesn't come, minutes are passing.

She finally appears in the doorframe holding a smoke, tossing me one. "Marissa is right, Arch. I can't make you do this to you. I have to go home and face my fate."

What the bloody hell is that supposed to mean? "I want you to stay Hayley."

Her body tenses a tiny bit whenever I say her name. "Do you have feelings for her?"

I let out a tiny puff of air. When I told her we dated, I never told her the truth. It seemed like she never cared much. Out of everything that's happened today, she is only caring about what Marissa has said. "We went on one date. We left early because it was bloody awkward."

She nods, puffing on her fag she looks lost in thought. I think I'm losing her.

"Don't go. If you do, then I'm following you."

She falls on the bed ignoring my plea. "I can't go back to New York. Once we are married, I need to stay here."

I sit up scooting to sit beside her. "What are you running from?"

She looks up at me, her eyes are starting to gloss over. "It's who I'm running from."

Her eyes land on my lips, then she leans in to kiss me. It was just a sweet innocent kiss.

I look into her eyes smiling, she has no idea how happy she makes me. I tuck her wet hair behind her ear. "No one was around."

She looks up at me. Our gaze meets and it feels like everything around us just combust into flames. "I just needed it."

She smiles, giving me the same excuse, I gave her when I kissed her.

Her eyes gaze to the pillow. "It's bedtime. There's been too much confession for one day."

I scoot back to my side of the bed not taking my eyes off her. "Do you want me to hold you again?"

Siren nods, wiping a stray tear rolling down her face. "I want to spend time with your mom before we get married. I have to apologise to her for taking your future away."

I grab her gently, pulling her down to me. She did way too good of a job pretending that getting slammed into a wall never hurt her this morning. "You aren't stealing anything from me."

Little does she know I'm holding the only future I have in my arms.

Chapter 12

Hayley

When I told Archie I wanted to spend time with his mom, I was talking about having a short dinner with just the three of us, possibly a day before we go to the courthouse. I was not talking about just me and her sitting in her living room together drinking tea pretending I like it.

The tension she is giving off is a bit insulting. She hasn't relaxed her shoulders since I walked in. Basically, sitting in a room with her sums up my relationship with both Josh's and Spencer's fathers. Tense, hatred, mix in a lot of awkwardness and you have the perfect mix of my teenage years.

Her living room is the best of the best. I can feel the high price tag of the soft velvet couch against my bare legs. The walls are painted a nice relaxing pastel blue. The lamps in the corners of the room are from Neiman Marcus. I'm not one hundred percent sure, but the dress she is wearing looks a lot like it's from Chanel. I feel bad for not really paying attention to her the first two times I met her, my mind was in another place. I never noticed the amount of Botox injected into her face. She is trying to look younger, it almost makes her look older.

She looks down at my full teacup that is being hugged by my hands. "You're not a fan of tea, are you?" Her accent makes her sound like she is floating on clouds.

I look down at the steam coming out of the cup. "I'm a fan of coffee more or less."

She gives me a small smile. Both of us are stuck on what to say to each other. How can I blame her? My mom had big hopes and dreams for me, I can guarantee she has or had the same for her son.

I turn my head looking across the room onto the mantel or the fireplace, looking at a picture of Archie when he was a baby. He has the same aqua blue eyes, chubby cheeks and only a few strands of hair. Next to that is a picture of Archie, his mom and Alfie sitting around a Christmas tree. He can't be older than four. Down the line, the pictures eventually stop, but before they do, something in her smile changes and Alfie is completely out of the images.

My dad moved, he separated his life from my mom to try and keep her a secret. His words repeated in my head. My stomach turns, I'm terrified he is going to pack up one day and leave me behind. He is the only good thing in my life right now. If he packs up and leaves me behind, even if it's just for appearance I am going to slowly continue to die inside. The parts of me he saved me from are going to be ripped away. I can't let that happen.

The room is silent. I can hear her arrhythmic heartbeat from the matching chair on the other side of the room.

I set my cup down on the oak table in front of me, turning my head to look at her. "I just want you to know that me marrying Archie isn't what it looks like. It's genuine."

She looks at me, her body relaxes, her shoulders drop.

"I know this isn't the life he deserves. I do want to be with him."

Thirty looks of shock rush over her face. "He told you? You love him."

I wasn't expecting her to catch on like that. I was expecting her to just take it as I have feelings for him. It feels so nice for someone other than the guys to know how I feel about him, even if it's his mother.

Before I have time to respond to her the door opens. "Sorry. I had to deal with something." Archie shuts the door behind him walking towards us.

Whatever he had to deal with, it went south. He tried to clean himself up. He left a tiny drop of blood on his neck. I pat the couch beside me, pulling out a napkin dipping it in my tea. He sits and I wipe the blood off his neck. With the haunting look in his eyes, even if there wasn't a trace of blood left behind, I would know he killed someone.

He looks down at the napkin wide-eyed, his face lost all his colour. "I'm so sorry Siren. I-I."

Archie is stumbling over his words. He told me he wanted to keep me as far away as he could from everything. I know how everything works, so I didn't believe him when he told me. He can try yes, just because he tries doesn't mean it will work. It's harder than that. You need someone to lean on.

Liam and I always worked together, he was my right-hand guy. I think that's the only reason why we were together, and the only reason why he is doing his own absurd plan to get me back. Archie needs me to be the one that's there for him without me making it obvious I know exactly how he's feeling.

I drop the napkin on the table, fixating my gaze on him. It's been a few days since he shaved, so his facial hair is growing, there's a lot more than I find attractive. It's different on him. He is still as easy on the eyes as before. "Don't hide from me."

Archie grabs my hand, intertwining his fingers with mine. Moments like this, my mind goes to another place about him finding a reason to touch me. Right now, he just needs me to be with him, even if he thinks I don't understand why.

I see his mom looking at us. She is happy. She is as happy as Kinsley was when she saw me and Liam together. Archie touching me never sent my mind into thoughts about him having feelings for me, but the way his mother is smiling, the proud look in her eyes. That is what makes me think that Archie feels the exact same way as I do.

I want to cave and tell him how I feel. If I do, I need to tell him everything about the Basilisks. It wouldn't be fair for me to pile that onto him. I also know it's not fair for me to stay mute about it either. If I was him, I would want to know everything. I just need more time to process opening up myself to him.

"You don't have an engagement ring." Archie's mom stands up, walking out of the room.

I whisper. "What the hell is your mom's name?"

Archie laughs sending my favourite melody through my mind. "Olivia."

"Okay, where did *Olivia* go?"

Archie shrugs, making his hand tighten. Both of us look down, it feels so natural to me touching him, I forgot our fingers are intertwined with each other.

Olivia walks out with her hand in a fist. "This was Archie's grandma's. I was saving it for the right girl, I wasn't expecting it to be you."

She opens her hand revealing a dainty diamond on a silver band. My head is light, my throat is dry. I want to cry. I can't take it, I can't let that ring sit on my hand when I'm not being honest with him. If love was enough, I would take it, I can't let it sit on my finger when I'm full of lies.

Archie takes it from her without a single hesitation. His eyes are beaming. He is feeling the opposite that I am. "What do you say, Siren? Save it for our wedding day?"

Who would have guessed that a single ring can make me feel so guilty? How can one piece of jewellery make this so much more real? "I want you to save it for someone else. I can't accept it."

Archie stuffs the ring in his pocket. "If you think I'm doing this again, you're mad."

"Hayley, take it. Believe me, you are the only one who deserves to wear it." Olivia's tone is almost matching Archie's. The happiness in both of their voices is hard to miss.

"Let me see it." I hold out my hand palms up.

Archie digs in his pocket.

I slip it on my ring finger on my left hand. "It's a little big, we need to go resize it."

This is when I'm supposed to kiss him. I can feel the magnetic force working against us. I look down at it, not wanting to take the ring off. I pull out my phone, snapping a picture of it. I need to show my very pissed off brothers.

They are trying to support me the best they can, they are trying to understand. Spencer is understanding more than Josh is. I think Josh is trying to purposely not understand. We have been together every day since I was born, we are as close as twins are. He and Spencer have started clinging to each other more in my absence, trying to cling on to the thought of me coming back. I haven't told them about my decision to stay away from New York. I wasn't sure I was serious about staying away. Not until I got this family aplomb on my finger.

I need to take a step back and look at everything. Me going back home made no sense. I was walking into a death trap. I love Archie, I need to stay in case he is in love with me too. I need to stay here for him, I can't risk not coming back. I can't be the one to let eight people shatter.

I take off the ring, open up my purse, put it in the smallest pocket and zippering it up so it will stay safe. "Everything is going to work out. I promise."

I say the words out loud making Archie and Olivia think I'm saying it to them. I'm really trying to convince myself I'm not making a horribly huge mistake.

I drop my purse looking at the mantel. Images flash through my mind of our future with just the two of us. I feel joy at first, then everything but. "You need to promise me you will never move out." I look at Olivia in the chair apologising for the words I'm about to say. "We can't do this if we live apart."

Archie grabs my hand again. "I can't think of anything worse."

Chapter 13

Archie

Jack falls on the couch under him. "Your girlfriend is weird, mate." He is staring at the painting. "Why is there a unicorn in your living room?"

I shake my head. "It's a ship."

"You and your girlfriend are both screwed up." He points to his head.

Now that she has met Jack, I have been a little worried she was going to change her mind about whatever it is we are doing. He is more her type. He is covered in tattoos and his hair is a lot similar to William, Spencer and Josh. He is built like me. I need to believe in her more. He walks in and she doesn't bat an eye. I am overthinking everything once again when it comes to her. Most of all, I need to believe in my friend who I am in life and death situations with almost every single day.

"The only thing I can think of is killing Alfie. Call the police and say he was going to shoot me. I'll go to jail. I can't leave her behind." I tip my head back on the couch, my mind is so tired of thinking of the same dead-end options.

"You would kill your father?" The astonishment in Jack's voice is reminding me of everything I hate in myself.

"She's my weakness, he knows that. I need Siren to be okay."

"If you kill him, someone else is going to step up."

That is also my other worry. I know Cartels don't end. Everyone involved would be arrested. I glance over at my business textbooks on the kitchen counter. Being in University is a waste of time. I'm never going to be able to use my degree. If I stay out of jail long enough to graduate.

Jack pulls out his phone. "I'm calling Ava, she's a bitch, but she's good in bed. Do you want me to get Mia over here for you mate?"

I glare at Jack. Mia was the one girl I would call whenever I was bored, she never complained. She would come over, then leave right after there wasn't any cuddling, or making plans for tomorrow. It was nice, easy and fucking simple.

The door opens, I don't need to look at the clock to know Sirens last class of the week is finished.

"I have tequila and limes! I don't know about you guys, but I need a fuckin' drink." She walks around the couch into the living room kicking Jack as she walks by.

Jack looks at me, with a broad grin. "Am I calling Mia or what?" His voice is loud enough for each word to be heard where Siren is standing.

Her shoulders drop. My attention is brought down to the ring finger on her left hand. It's only been three days, but they got her ring sized. I thought she was going to wait to wear it. Jack is still staring at me, I can see his beady eyes from the corner of my eye, staring at me. He's waiting for me to say out loud in front of Siren that I only want her. If this was any other girl, I'd say "Call her." She isn't any other girl. Hayley Cohen has fucked my mind up. Her wearing the ring is my case and point. How is she casually wearing it? Most of all what the hell was said between her and Mum for her to give her my Grandma's ring?

Siren unwraps the bottle of tequila, setting it on the counter. "Arch, you have other bedrooms for me to sleep in?" She twists off the lid of the bottle, then reaches into the cupboard pulling shot glasses down and pours all of us a shot. Siren puts the glass to her lips knocking it back. "I can't tell you not to have girls over."

I look at the floor, I don't want to look in her eyes and see whatever it is I'm going to be looking into. "How do you expect me to think about that when you're wearing your ring?"

The drawer opens and closes.

Jack stands, I grab his arm tightly as he walks by. "Don't bloody bring her here."

Jack snorts. "Do you think I have a death wish?"

I look back up at Siren, she's gripping the counter with her left hand as if it's the only thing keeping vertical. Her right hand is gripping the neck of the bottle. I stand shuffling my feet to her. It feels like we are always walking on the gates of hell with each other. I want to talk, I can never find the words. I get closer, her left ring finger is naked.

I open the drawers, looking for it. I open the one she is hovering over searching under her body. I found the right one. She isn't moving, making this harder on both of us. We both clearly feel the same way about one another. I opened up to her, she just won't do the same.

The dainty diamond is under my fingertips. I wrap my hand around it, pulling my arm back to my body. "Put it back on Siren."

I fight the bottle out of her hands pouring myself a shot. I raise the shot glass to my mouth, instantly regretting it. I close my eyes tight, trying not to gag. I can hear her shuffling around and something cool is touching my lips. My taste buds are calming down with the bitterness.

She shoved a bloody lime in my mouth.

She bought limes for me, not her.

Humiliated.

"Try taking it as a body shot later. I don't know if it's the salt or the sexual part of it. It just makes it better." Siren looks up at me with her downward turned eyes, they're bigger than normal. She's searching for something.

The muscles in my face are fighting against each other to force my smile into a frown. Sleeping with her is a bad idea, this is a bad idea too. She planted the idea in my head, so I am going to take full advantage of this.

I open my hand, listening to the ring land on the counter making a small *cling* noise, I push it towards her. "Put your ring on. You don't get to try to sleep in another one of our bedrooms while I bang a girl who means nothing to me."

She keeps saying your house, your food, she's even asking if she can shower. I don't know how to keep explaining to her that it's her house now just as much as it is mine. She's a permanent visitor.

I walk to the living room. "Help me move furniture. Jack is going to turn this place into a party. We need a dance floor."

I turn back around watching her slip her ring over her finger. I have a week to go buy us a wedding band. Thankfully, I was there when she was sized so I know her ring size. This is the farthest thing from a sham wedding, we are just doing everything backwards. She looks happier, at least on the outside. She doesn't tell me much. I pay attention enough to know her mind is always screaming at her.

Twenty minutes later, the couches are pushed against the walls and music is playing through the speakers. People are piling in. There's not as many as I expected Jack to reel up, just a few people from school. I don't know how I'm supposed to do this, she doesn't know anyone. She doesn't give anyone the chance to know her. When she's around people she's quiet, she watches everyone from a distance. It's almost like she is expecting the worst from people she doesn't know.

There aren't many sober people, Siren and I are one of the few only ones that won't be ready for bed in an hour. I check her out, looking to see what she's wearing. I need to play this properly. I only have one chance to try to win her over tonight. I need to not screw this up. Her tight tank top is going to make this extremely easy.

I grab her hand, dragging her into the kitchen. "Move your hair from your neck and tip your head."

She scrunches her nose. Siren bites her bottom lip, doing as I say.

Holy shit. I turn around not letting my excitement knock me on my ass. I pull out the salt from the seasoning rack. I turn around filling a shot glass to the brim, I grab a sliced lime slipping it between her teeth. Then I reach for the salt sprinkling it on her neck and place the shot glass between her boobs.

My dick is already hard, and I haven't even touched her skin yet.

I lean down licking the salt off her neck, trying to make it as seductive as I can. She lets out a tiny moan. I kiss her neck where the trail of salt ends. I bend down even farther, wrapping my lips around the shot glass, placing my hands on her hips, I tip the tequila back. Siren takes the shot glass from my mouth taking a step closer to me. I take the lime from her mouth.

She's breathing hard.

I move my hand from her hip, pulling the lime out of my mouth and our lips crash together. I'm not even sure who kissed who. This is the neediest, sloppiest, lust hungry kiss I have ever experienced in my life.

She pulls away, hitting her hand against my chest. "Damn it."

I wrap my arms around her lower back, pulling her into me even closer. I need to lay the cards on the table. "I love you."

She laughs once with a smile batting me away. "Shut up. No one can hear you."

I drop my hands from her waist walking away. She is the most infuriating woman I have ever come across. She is too damaged for her own good. There's only one type of person that would accept my lifestyle so easily. She is just as fucked up as I am, if not more.

There's one huge difference between us. I'm going to dig until I find out what she's hiding from in New York.

Siren's voice is being washed out from the music. I look over my shoulder. I trust them both, so I don't understand why I have a burning pit of jealousy in my belly seeing her so close to Jack, or any other guy. I get closer to her to hear her speak, "Get everyone out of here."

Jack looks past her over to me.

I nod. I place my hand on Siren's back. "You alright?"

She doesn't say anything. She takes my hand leading me up the stairs, down the hall and backs up into our bedroom.

I shut the door listening to people being rounded up. "What is going on?"

Siren places her hand on my chest. I can feel her pulse from his wrist. The look in her eyes is sexy as hell. My plan worked.

"Arch, I—"

Before she can finish I lean into her lips kissing her. Siren's hands travel to my jeans unsnapping the button. She takes a step back, unsnaps the buttons of her high waisted jeans, pulls her tucked in tank top over her head.

I've been daydreaming about what she looked like naked. I had no idea how toned her abs were. I knew she worked out, and she's fit. I never thought I would see outlines of abs on her. I frantically rip the shirt off my body, watching her soak in every detail of me shirtless. I walk up to her unsnapping her bra from behind her back.

She walks away from me dropping her jeans to the ground. She is completely naked in front of my eyes. "Grab a condom, and fuck me, Arch."

I spin around on my heels reaching into my closet pulling down the box of condoms. I step out of my pants, giving Siren a gentle shove onto the bed.

She moves the pillows shoving them against the wall laying in the middle of the bed with her legs open and knees bent. I kneel on the bed leaning in for another kiss. My hand travels down her body, gropes her boob as I play with her nipple, feeling her back arch against my skin. Siren grabs my arm, squeezing it tight. I move my hand down farther, feeling her warmth on my fingers.

So, fucking tight.

She has short breaths against my lips, with every motion I make of my hand. I move my mouth from her lips, listening to her breathing hard I kiss her neck and collar blades. I move my mouth down to her nipples gently, running my teeth around them, feeling her body start to squirm under me. I move down, father pulling my finger out from inside her.

Hayley moans realising what I'm about to do. I feel her hand grab mine.

She's in love with me.

I stroke my tongue.

Hayley breathes deeply. "Archie, I want you. Please."

I sit up not waiting to argue. I look for the condom, she already has the corner ripped open holding it out for me. I look at her hand then back at her before taking it from her. She is so impatient. She showed it to me, making me grab it from her and put it on. I hover over her kissing her neck, slowly making my way into her.

Siren lets out a gasp as she stretches around me, then a loud moan. Her nails are already digging into my back. I keep slamming my hips against hers, I have no self-control. I can't try to make this last as long as I want. Her moaning is sending my brain into overdrive.

I lean back watching the panic strike in her eyes thinking I'm about to finish. I move her legs onto my shoulders, bending forwards, watching her eyes light up with another thrust.

"Hayley," Her name left my throat sounding like a growl. "You feel amazing."

Her eyes roll back in her head as her body begins to shake. "Fuck!"

I'm right behind her. My body tenses, my eyes lock on hers.

Siren touches my face. "I love you." The words are quieter than a whisper, I'm not even sure if I heard her right.

I fall onto the mattress beside her, not reacting to what she might or might not have said. I keep trying to tell myself that she was riding the wave of an orgasm, I know I am.

Siren sits up. "We shouldn't have done that. I shouldn't have done that." She turns to look at me with fear in her eyes. "Arch, I'm so sorry."

I know what I heard. She doesn't know I heard her. "A sexless marriage isn't good for anyone."

She looks at me giving me a small smile. "It's your fault. You had to go and kiss my neck. Worst best friend ever."

I glare at her while covering myself up with the blanket, I take the condom off. Siren doesn't put up a fight with me as I pull her perfect naked body against my naked body under the sheets.

I kiss her neck. "You shouldn't have told me."

Siren smacks my arm. "Shut up."

Hayley Cohen fucking loves me.

Chapter 14

Hayley

Why I was so insistent on sleeping with Archie is beyond me. Well, it's really not. He's perfect in every single way possible. I've only ever had sex with him and Liam and they both blew me out of the water. Liam was so careful with me, but Archie has lust written all over his face. It was like that's all he has been thinking about.

Not to say I haven't been trying to put his mind there. I ventured from baggy sweaters to tight tank tops hoping to pull his eyes on me. It worked a hell of a lot better than I thought it was going to.

Sex with Archie is still leaving me lost for words. I was stupid enough to mutter *I love you*. Who does that? Who the hell does that? I wanted to cry, hell I still do. I act like I never said it, he's trying to pretend with me. Us pretending doesn't change the fact that something between us changed for the worst.

I don't know what's worse: pretending like I never told him, or saying it and him brushing it off. It's not like I wanted him to find out I'm truly in love with him after he gave me a life-changing orgasm. It was probably my two-year streak without sex being broken that was life changing and not so much the sex. But I doubt it.

The only person I can call and brag to is April. I can't even do that, she's Liam's big sister. It would make things awkward. I have to deal with this cluster fuck of feelings and thoughts in my head alone.

I walk downstairs falling onto the couch next to Jack. I don't know what is so different about me. He is everything I would be attracted to; Tattoos, the hair, his smile, I'm not going to lie, his ass is the definition of perfection. He just doesn't do it for me. He's attractive. I think he is too much of a resemblance to the Basilisks, his relationship with the Cartel is too much of a flashback for me.

"You look like a train wreck."

I shiver. No wonder I'm not attracted to him, he's like my bothers. "I have a lot going on in my head."

"Does sex normally mess girls up this much?" He laughs. "I hope not. I'd feel bad."

"You're revolting," I say simply.

He shrugs, just like William would have. I let out a sigh that sounds more like a cry. Somehow this one person is reminding me of three people all at once. I can see him looking at me from the corner of his eye muffling a laugh. Being friends with guys has always been easier for me, it's what I know. It is a natural friendship between us. There isn't any awkwardness like he's choosing either me or Archie. Ron and I are awkward all around.

"Jack, I need you to be honest with me. Why didn't Rose share the door with you in the ocean?"

I cover my face with my arms right as soon as he smacks me across the head with the back of his hand. "You're a fucking twit."

I cackle.

"Your boyfriend puts up with a lot, doesn't he?"

I stop laughing while picking at my shirt.

"Bloody hell mate."

I lean back into the couch. At this point, everyone other than Archie is going to know how I feel about him. I feel cornered when it comes to people in his life raising questions about him.

Archie yells from the railing upstairs, I thought he was in class. He *should* be in class. "When Siren comes home can you let me know?"

I spin around grabbing the back of the couch. "You call me that even when I'm not around?" My voice ended up being more of a shriek than anything.

Archie's footsteps are hitting the floors in fast motions until he is standing in front of me with his hands in his pockets. I toss him a smoke and he lets out a small puff of air. Ever since I let those three little words slip from my mouth he has been acting standoffish. He's been trying to be nice about it, Archie has just been so distant.

It is starting to destroy me. Not letting it show when I live with him is hard. Somehow, I've been managing.

"Oh, this is going to be good," Jack smirks. He waves his hand in the space between Archie and I, "Continue."

Archie glares at Jack, I can feel his laser beams from the cushion next to me. "Eh? Siren come upstairs. I need to show you something."

I try not to hesitate. Anything could be waiting for me up there. I get up despite the dreaded conversation that we are going to have. It is going to happen sooner or later. I just need to get it over with.

I pause halfway up the stairs. My stomach is turning, I'm dreading everything about this. "Arch, I'm sorry for the other night. I didn't want you to be acting like this. This is all my fault."

He turns around reaching down for my hand pulling me up the stairs. "I'm an adult. I can handle sleeping with my best friend."

He drags me down the hall opposite his bedroom to the spare room. "If you don't start calling this place your house too, I'm going to go mad as a bag of ferrets."

Archie swings open the door. The single bed that was in here has been replaced. I walk in looking at the wooden art easel with a bar stool in front, a six-section shelf is connected to the wall with paints lined up. Sitting next to an art easel is a wooden desk with a brand-new brush set sitting safely in a black velvet case. The curtains are taken off the wall to let the natural light shine in.

I turn around, looking behind me. Archie is standing next to the photo I painted of him. I guess he found out I really didn't have to hand it in.

I put my hands up to my chest. No one has ever done something like this for me before. I spin back around looking at the room shocked. I turn back again, "You did this for me?"

"I suck at keeping secrets. It wasn't about you seducing me."

I run up to him reaching up to wrap my arms around his neck. I give him a kiss on the cheek, trying not to linger. "Thank you."

Archie holds me against his body, holding me tighter than ever. If he never heard me, I will be able to make it right this time. I need to find a moment when I'm not coming down from mind-blowing sex, and when it's just the two of us.

"We are getting married tomorrow." Archie pulls away, his five o'clock shadow rubbing against my face. "I'm not writing you vows."

I smirk. "Good, me either."

I walk away gathering everything I need to paint from my newfound inspiration.

Archie Upton.

All of the artwork I create from now on is going to be pulled from him, and our not so fake future together.

Chapter 15

Archie

Standing outside the courthouse with my wedding band on my left hand has me feeling like the luckiest guy in the world, even with the reasons we got married. Sirens face when I pulled out the wedding band for her to give me, she lit up. It was like every expectation was met.

That is complete bollocks. The courthouse wedding, casual clothes, a surprise wedding band. None of this is what she wanted. No one she loves from America is here, this is supposed to be her special day. Her parents aren't here, no one is here for her. I never noticed until now, she may have been running from something, but I stole her wedding day right out from under her feet. I was so panicked about what happens next that I forgot about Siren.

Siren touches my face with her hand. "Arch you alright?"

I look into her serene eyes, the guilt only weighs down on me more. She deserved so much better than this. She deserved the wedding of her dreams. I know she needed help, I did that, I helped her. She lost so much in the process. How am I supposed to ever apologise for that?

I reach down to her left hand with my fingertips on her rings. "It's just a lot to take in."

"I know. I'm sorry. One day you can have the wedding and the life that you deserve."

I stand staring at her. The tone in her voice, this has been haunting her. The thoughts never came to me until now, but they have been in her mind since probably the beginning. It is scary how well she holds herself together.

I need to hire a PI. I should have done it weeks ago. If she was able to fake a smile around me while her thoughts destroyed her, I couldn't imagine who she is running from. I lean down brushing my lips across her lips. Siren kisses me, pulls away and cuddles up in my chest.

"Arch, isn't that your dad?"

I look over to my left. He is walking towards us alone. I turn my back whispering, "Call Jack, get him to pick you up."

Siren looks up at me nodding slowly, almost as if this was nothing new to her. This is the hell I was worried about. I watch her walk away into a crowd of people. Turning around, Dad has his gaze on her as well.

Dad moves his hands out to the side. "I only came to congratulate you, son, no need to send her away."

I glance back to the federal building. This is no place to have this conversation. "Meet me at mums."

***

I'm not the type of person to run to their mum for protection. I have no idea where Dad lives, and I'm sure as hell not bringing him back to my place.

I lean against the wall, frustrated and already exhausted. "What do you want?"

"Now that you are married, I pass it down to you."

I push myself from the wall with my foot. "And if I don't you kill her." I pause, thinking about me having to shoot Jeremy. "If you aren't soft enough to let it stop you."

Dad's eyes flick with rage glaring out of them. "You have lost the plot because of her. Baker men don't give up their family inheritance for love."

"I guess it's a good thing I'm not a Baker man now isn't it?"

If I was armed, I would shoot him right here, not second thinking about the consequences. I would turn myself over to the police and finish this, let them take all of us down, one by one.

"Fourteen days, until you step up and be a man, or you let her die." He walks out of the house slamming the door behind him.

I fall back into the wall. "Fuck!"

I push myself from the wall to see Siren staring at me, her body is shaking. *Why the bloody hell did I do this to her?* I reach out to her, pulling her into my body. She's like a rag doll, Siren has lost all control of her limbs.

"Babe, I'm going to protect you. I'm so sorry."

"I knew he wanted me dead." She pushes out of my arms. Her skin is ice cold. "Let me kill him." Her voice is lower than I ever thought possible.

I shake my head, trying to see if I processed her words properly. *Who the fuck am I married to?* I sidestep heading out the front door. I needed a PI a month ago.

Hayley

Why did I say that? Oh. My. God. The Basilisk in me, the cold-hearted murder just came out. Archie's face, I never thought I could see a Cartel member so terrified. I can see Archie on the phone pacing back and forth, I wouldn't put it past him if he's already trying to get me back to New York. The words slipped out. My survival instincts kicked in. Everything I have worked so hard to run away from fell on my lap in a blink of an eye and I took it.

I need a smoke. Walking to the front door I hesitate, I really don't want to hear Archie's phone call. I don't want to face him. I open the door anyway, I live with him, and I'm married to him. As much as I would like to, I can't hide from him.

"Yes. Thank you." He hangs up the phone looking at me. "How much of that did you hear?"

I light my smoke, my hand is shaking. The fear of losing everything is too real right now. "I just got outside."

He's standing on the pathway studying my face like I'm his fucking business textbooks. "Are you going to tell me who you are now?" He points to the house. "That was fucked up, Hayley."

My eyes are burning from my tears. I want to tell him more than ever. Everything just gets more screwed up. Two separate organised crime groups want me dead. That isn't something people take lightly, or at all. There's nothing to say so I don't say anything at all.

"Get your shit out of the bedroom. I was honest about everything. You are choosing not to believe in me right now. Get your own bloody ride home."

My chest is closing in on me, making it hard to speak. "Your mom's having people over for us."

"Do you really think I could pretend to be in love with you right now?"

I turn around putting my smoke out before leaving it in the ashtray. He knew that would cut me, he did it on purpose. I open the door, wishing Jack had just taken me to his place like I told him to. My chest is heaving, I can hardly take a full breath. Archie has every right to be pissed off at me, he just didn't have a right to remind me he doesn't love me when he knows exactly how I feel about him.

I give myself half a second to collect my emotions before walking into the kitchen to grab my purse. "I don't mean to run out. I'm not feeling very good and not much in a party mood." I'm trying to make my voice as cheerful as I can, walking back to Olivia and Jack.

There is no point in lying, there's an open window and by the looks on both their faces, they were both listening.

The lies keep coming, even though I know it's useless. "I have a few projects due soon, I don't think I'll be able to attend next weekend."

Olivia's face sinks. "I wanted you to help set it up."

I nod. If this is going to work out between me and Archie, I need to try to do some normal people things. Even if that includes setting up a bloody ball.

"Let me drive you mate." Jack stands up from the kitchen table.

"She can find her own way home."

I back away, wiping an escaped tear from my eye. "Have fun husband."

Archie hits his hand on the counter. I turn to walk away expecting him to chase after me or call my name. He doesn't. I need to figure out the address and find a way to get home.

Hell, this is reminding me a lot of Spencer and Cameron's story.

Chapter 16

Archie

I'm gone to the dogs. I have never been more disappointed in myself and my mum had the most disappointed look on her face. I should have chased after Siren, I should have thrown her over my shoulder, sat her down and told her exactly how I feel. I should have never let her run away from me like that.

I'm not even sure if she's eating, she doesn't come out of her room other than for class. I think she waits for me to leave until it's safe for her to come out. This isn't what I expected married life to be like. I've been checking her artwork, it's the only way I can communicate with her. I have no idea what they mean, I just know they are dark.

Looking at them, I wouldn't have guessed the happy, laughing girl that is now hiding in her room painted any of these. I sit at her stool, I'm desperate. I live in the same house as her, my bed is ten feet away from hers and I can't see her, or talk to her, or bloody apologise. I get off the stool walking over to the shelf's full of paint, searching for a lighter colour that has been open.

I pick up a light blue colour. She only ever wears blue, this has to be it. I pop open the cap and groan when the foil is still on. I begin to open every single bottle. The foil is the same for the first three, then four and five. I pick up the sixth bottle, opening the cap seeing traces of dried bright pink paint on the cap. I tip my head back letting out a sigh. I don't know how I'm going to do this, all I know is touching an artist's painting, is going to get my hand broken.

I squirt a little bit on the round circle thing with paint already on it, I drip my brush and write out the words *I'm sorry*. The black streaks are dark enough making the hot pink colour reflect off it.

What the bloody hell did she use pink for? I stand up, walking over to the wall looking through her artwork that is leaning against one another. None of this is making any sense to me. She doesn't do something without a reason. I start from the back looking at two silhouettes who I'd imagine to be us. Their foreheads are touching. Above the silhouettes, there is an unsettling large snake with red eyes hovering. The one in front of that is a wall dividing the canvas into two separate rooms. There is a girl leaning against the wall and in the other room, there are two people in bed.

I keep flipping through. The next is a black canvas with the number one in a circle and her name in dark red paint.

My stomach is flipping. I can't do this anymore.

My phone rings making my heart slam against my chest. "Hello?"

"I looked into Hayley Cohen. I'm sending you back your money. I can't help you." The line disconnects.

I stand in the middle of the art room spooked from the paintings, the PI I hired is giving me a full refund. Who the hell is she?

"What are you doing in here?" I turn around to the sound of Hayley's voice. She is hugging her middle.

Her eyes are drawn to the pictures behind me.

"I didn't know how else to talk to you."

"Please get out Archie. I didn't realise you were home. I would have stayed in my room."

I never thought it was possible to see someone so broken. I was purposely trying to hurt her. Once again, I wasn't thinking about her. I wasn't thinking about the time frame my Dad put on her life and I sure as hell wasn't thinking about whatever the fuck she was painting.

"Can we please talk?"

She looks up at me with the most heartbroken look in her eyes. I can feel the heaviness of her chest from five feet away. "You don't have to pretend to love me. We both know I don't have much time left and I can't be with the people who really love me, so just leave me the fuck alone."

Right now, arguing with her is completely useless. I'm fighting every bone in my body to walk away from her. "Give me five minutes, that's all I need to keep you safe."

I storm past her not waiting for the look of realisation across her beautiful, broken face. I jog down the hall into the bedroom, locking the door and falling onto my bed taking out my phone. I still have time to buy, I just need to do something not selfish for Siren for once.

"Have you decided, son?" Dad's voice is enough to trigger my rage.

"I still have ten days. Give me those ten days and I will be the Baker Cartel boss."

"Ten days." The line disconnects.

Siren is pounding on the door. "Archie no!"

I fly up from the bed unlocking the door, opening it to see the look of panic strike my wife's face. "I have a plan."

"What is it?"

"I have ten days to figure it out. You have a lifetime Siren."

She turns white, all of the colours are left from her face and a sob leaves her lips. "Call him back. He can take me right now, just call him back."

I place my hand on her cheek. She closes her eyes leaning into my hand. "He'll be dead before then. You will get deported, but you'll be alive."

"Why would you go through with marrying me?"

Now is the time I need to lay everything down. I can't find the words, none are coming to me.

"Archie," Her voice turns into a whine. Her eyes are saying what I couldn't. She knows I love her.

"Come to bed. It's been lonely without you."

She follows me in laying down, neither of us cares that it's only five. This room hasn't felt like my bedroom without her next to me. Whatever her secret is, I don't care. We will handle it when she tells me.

As soon as Siren's body hit our mattress, she fell asleep. I kiss her head. "I love you."

I could stay as boss, it would be the easier route. I could keep her here in London and we could be as happy and as in love as we could be under the circumstances. Or I could kill my own father.

I close my eyes tight. The answer is laying, asleep in my arms. I'm the new boss, and there's nothing I can do to stop it. I'm not giving her up for anything. My blind rage isn't worth the risk.

Siren rolls over her face is only inches from mine. "You need to do this Arch. I can't be without you."

I look down and her eyes are closed. She let off a small smile, she finally heard me. I rest my head against hers, wrapping my arms tighter around her.

Love can really fuck a man up.

Chapter 17

Hayley

"Adam, what do you mean?" I take a deep breath running my hands through my hair, looking across the courtyard staring at Archie while he talks to Ron.

"Hayley, you are on the top of our list. We tried to work slowly." I can only imagine the look in Adam's eyes. He's to caring for his own good.

I can hear William, Liam, Dillon, Spencer and Josh swearing. Their voice is echoing, they must be in Martin's office.

"We never told him where you are, as far as we know none of us knows where you are, and no one has spoken to you."

"It won't take long for him to find out. Damn it." Why I thought it was a good reason to run away is beyond me at this point. "I have to go." I hang up the phone, stuffing it back in my purse.

I'm lightheaded, it feels like I'm going to faint. Running away did me absolutely no benefit. The Basilisk hitmen are too good. We move through lists faster than we should, and Martin is in a hurry. He put the most time into me, making my skills as perfect as he could. Me leaving was a personal attack to him, saying enough is enough. Men like Martin Taylor don't like weakness, if he could he would reach into someone's heart the moment any weakness is shown, and rip out their heart. That's why he is going to send people I don't have a relationship with. He knows Josh, Spencer and William found me.

"Fuck." I raise both hands to my head. I'm lucky to have a week left. It's not going to take long for them to find me.

I obviously don't have a gun here. I have no way to protect myself against Martin's brainwashed minions. A part of me is hoping that one of my "fathers" show up. Maybe once in their life, they will have some sort of weakness for me. That's exactly why Martin isn't going to send them.

I've never been so fucked in my life.

"Siren. What did Adam say?" Archie places his hands on my hips pulling me into his body. "We will get through it alright?"

I fall into his chest, closing my eyes. I know he went through my artwork. I should be absolutely furious. I'm not. Even though it's equivalent to reading my diary I don't feel an ounce of resentment. At least now he knows something is wrong. I painted the hit list with my name in a desperate cry for him to see it. The silhouette was painted the day he gave me my art room. I painted that hoping he would see us in it, the snake was added so he knew someone was going to be controlling us.

I don't know how to tell him in words, painting is the only language I can communicate in.

"I'll keep my wife safe. Just tell me what the bloody hell is going on." He holds me tighter.

I have completely forgotten we are at school. My mind slips away from my repairing heart. Everything in this moment feels the exact way it should. On the outside it looks that way too, just a husband and wife soaking in each other's embrace, you would never guess what lives we are actually living.

I grab onto his shirt. "Are you pretending to love me? Is this all an act?"

Archie takes a step back looking down at me. "It never was an act. I knew how you felt. I wanted to get under your skin, make you angry enough to finally tell me everything."

I knew that, I just needed to know if he was going to be honest with me.

Marissa bounces towards us. I haven't seen her since Archie left with me at the pub, I don't think Archie has even spoken to her since then. His body relaxes, stepping away from me giving her a hug. They are whispering something to each other. I thought I would feel a sense of jealousy or something when this moment happened, I don't. Archie made it clear to me that there was never anything there for him, I have to trust him on this.

Marissa smiles watching Archie wrap his arm around me pulling me into his body. "Are you still coming to the hair appointment tomorrow with me and Ava?"

"No. I need to help Olivia set up. I probably won't have a chance to get ready."

Marissa raises her eyebrows. "She asked me one year and she never even showed."

I shrug. "I can't bail. I'm not sure how much she likes me at the moment. I'll just see you there."

Marissa wanders off and Archie looks down at me speaking in a low voice. "The only person my mom doesn't like right now is my Dad. I'm walking you to class Mrs Upton."

I nod with a smile. I hate my new last name. Hayley Upton? What is that? It sounds like an apartment building or a five-star hotel. I also hated dealing with the loads of paperwork I had piled on me in the middle of our fight. I am never going to be fighting with Archie again, it's too painful. It's even worse when he apologises by agreeing to become a boss.

Why the hell does Liam have a plan of becoming a boss to save me and now Archie is stuck in that same fate? I suck the life out of everything. I feel as if loving me is a sure-fire way to fuck up your life, so far, I am the only common denominator in both of them losing any chance they ever had.

I walk holding onto him tighter. Archie does the same to me silently, reassuring me. It's like our minds are thinking about the same thing right now. Saying I wish I never met him, so he could avoid his fate seems harsh and unavoidable. He is a Baker by blood, fate was going to land in his lap either way. I only sped up the process by making him marry me, by planting the seed in his mind.

Saying I'm sorry isn't enough. There is nothing I can do to try and fix this. I want Alfie dead as much as I want Martin dead. Killing either one of them is useless, someone else would step up. It would only take away the free days Archie has. Killing Martin would only take away Adam's free days.

Normally a Taylor becomes boss in the Basilisks, but they vote. Adam is young, he's relentless and he is mentally and physically strong. Unless someone else comes in, Adam is going to face the fate. Liam's plan is going to blow up in his face leaving him married to someone he will never love.

I stop tugging on Archie's arm. Pulling him down for a hug, "Things are about to get really messed up. Just remember that I love you."

He holds me tighter, this is the first time I ever said it loud enough for him to clearly hear with no one else around. We are backwards, we are married, and we just started dating. The speed of our relationship means nothing, the only thing that means anything is that we are handling two wars.

"Give me a chance to fight with you, and I will fight." Archie whispers, I think he is starting to put the pieces together.

Chapter 18

Hayley

My stomach is turning, staring at a white banner that readers *Fundraiser Ball for Children* in blue glitter. I have never been so disgusted in my life, I've heard of money laundering, I am not a stranger to it. Using children is a disgusting tactic and I am repulsed beyond words.

"The money actually goes to the children, Siren. My mom organises this every year." Archie places his hand on my back. "She hires security to keep us out."

I look around the room, seeing a high ceiling, large open windows with thin drapes covering them. The floor clicks under any footstep echoing off the walls, and onto the roof. Caters are lining into the building with portable food warms. Others are packing in trays, they are all wearing white and black uniforms. A DJ booth is set up in the back corner testing the sound.

I grab Archie's arm, taking the dress bag off his arm. "You're here though. They aren't doing a very good job."

Archie laughs with a warm smile on his face. "Me, Ron, Jack and a few others will be here. Mostly to make sure Alfie doesn't go back on his word. Just think of us as your own personal bodyguards."

Wonderful. "There's not much for me to set up."

The more I look around, there is nothing for me to set up. The banners are already hung, the caters are doing their jobs. The DJ has his own help hooking up the system into the speakers. This isn't a high school dance, so I'm assuming there won't be decorations to hang.

Archie looks around the room pulling out his phone from his sweater. "What is Siren expected to do? Yes, Mum. You could have—never mind. I'll see you later tonight." He looks at me puffing out a breath of air, stuffing his phone back in his sweater pocket. "Marissa never cancelled your hair appointment. We can still make it." He reaches down to grab my hand, stopping as his fingers start to trace the palm of my hand. "Mum didn't think you would forgive me and did everything in the past few days."

"Arch, I don't want this big fuss over me. I don't want my hair done and I sure as hell don't want bodyguards. I don't want a night of pretending. The clock is going to strike twelve and the daydream is going to be over."

Archie grabs my hand pulling me outside. I'm scared I have started a fight, or I'm about to start a fight. He has told me he feels like he walks on the ledge with me. Now I'm feeling that way, I'm scared I'm going to lose him, and next time I do I'm scared I'm going to lose him forever.

The sun is blinding, Archie stands in the way blocking the sun from my sight. "This is the worst first date ever." He raises his hand to his forehead.

The sound of cars driving by everyone who is on the sidewalk all their voices have turned into a loud roaring noise. The only difference between London and New York at this very minute is my surroundings.

Arch grins ear to ear. "Go home and change, do your hair and whatever else you girls do to get ready. We can leave really early and do something for ourselves. I don't care if it's a late-night tour bus or fast food."

If we would have communicated outside his mom's house like this, we never would have suffered through any of that pain. I can't believe I was going to find him a real date for tonight. It feels like forever ago. Those memories don't seem real anymore. Everything I learnt about Archie, all of my unanswered questions have been answered and I can't believe how much I love him. Every morning I wake up expecting all of this to be fake. Every single time he tells me he loves me it takes my brain a second to process it. We spent so much time pretending that it doesn't feel real.

I walk to the car, opening the door while watching Archie walk to the driver's side. "My dress is really easy to take off."

He hits the roof of the car with his fist, Archie has the biggest smile on his face. "I fucking love you, Hayley Upton."

***

My dress is hugging my hips, the cowl neckline is flattering to my athletic chest. The bright red dress and Archie's bright red tie is making this look like it was planned, even though we both know it wasn't. The ballroom looks nothing like I remember, we left with only a few people in here, each noise was amplified. Now with all these extra bodies, it isn't echoing. My voice isn't bouncing off every single surface.

Archie looks amazing. I'm used to guys in suits, but guys in tuxedos, he is making my heart skip a beat. I am married to the hottest guy in the room. The way he's looking at me, I know he is thinking the same thing. Or maybe he is trying to figure out how easy my dress really does come off. Either way, I'm the one that has taken over his mind, that's all I wanted.

The longer I stand here consumed by him, I can feel more people around me. I move my head looking off into the room. Everyone here is dressed up, men are all wearing tuxes, and women are wearing dresses. I would imagine this is what prom is like, except with older people and there's no one crying because they never got crowned queen.

"This is so much better than a friend date," Archie whispers in my ear, "I'm allowed to kiss you now."

"I can't dance, but dance with me Arch." I take his hand leading him to the dance floor.

My luck is that a slow song is on, there are no fancy moves. I have two left feet; it might be because I never had the chance to have a real dance with someone. Archie places his hands on my silk dress right on top of my hips pulling me into him. My arms are around his neck. We are almost the same high right now in my three-inch heels. His touch against the silk of my dress is better than I thought possible.

"Maybe you just never had the right dance partner." Archie has been avoiding asking about Liam, I think he's trying to dig.

I move my hands on his chest, lost in his eyes. I don't want to be talking about my ex right now, but if he needs me to reassure him, I will. I owe him that. "Not until you came along."

He grabs my hand, taking me a step back and spins me. My hair is flying around me, my toes are planted firmly on the ground letting him take control.

Archie pulls me into his body, putting his hands on my hips continuing to dance, while ignoring the stupid grin on my face. "Clearly he wasn't the one for you."

The song changes, it has a faster beat to it, neither of us is moving from each other's arms. Everything feels perfect. He has his arms wrapped around me and I'm feeling safer than I ever have before. Despite me being in more danger with him, I never felt so protected in my life.

The songs keep changing, but we are lost in one another. We had other plans for tonight, being in his arms until the music stops playing and we are the only ones on the dance floor feels so much better. This is our last year, after this, we can't come together and I'm going to be stuck on the side-lines thinking about this feeling. Thinking about his hands on my body. I can't think about that, I can deal with that next year and the year after. If I'm alive I will deal with it when the time comes. Right now, he is all I need to concentrate on.

"I know Siren, I'm going to miss this too." Archie kisses my hair resting his chin on my face, I don't know how he was able to read my mind.

I try to talk but all that comes out is a muffled cry against his tuxes jacket.

"I shouldn't have dragged you into this, I'm sorry."

I move my head looking up into his radiantly blue eyes. "You never dragged me into anything Arch."

I nuzzle my face back into his shoulder. How can two horrible people find each other and fall in love? It feels cruel that all this is happening, but really, it's karma designed for no one but us.

"Do you mind if I dance with him? We dance every year at these things." I turn around to look at Marissa.

I step back, this is their last year too. Archie reaches out for my left hand running his fingers over my engagement ring and wedding band. This was going to happen to Archie, the fate was already sealed for him, I only sped up the process because I never wanted to go back home. Everything he has now is fading away, all because of me.

Jack stands beside me passing me a tall cup full of bubbling champagne. I take a sip, knowing I already hate it. "Hayley, he'll be alright."

How is everyone reading my mind tonight? I step back standing to the side of the dance floor. "He's not keeping his life separate from me. I won't let him."

"He won't. Archie isn't Alfie." He shoves my shoulder. "I'm not sure who you are, but you're not Olivia."

We stand in silence absorbing the happiness from the room. This is a feeling that neither of us gets to experience very often. Archie and Marissa are both dancing and laughing, it's like they never got in a fight. He looks up at me, our eyes meet and instantly we both share a matching smile.

A normal person would feel resentment towards me. I would feel resentment towards Archie if the tables were turned. I even resent myself. He doesn't feel that way one bit.

It's scary as hell.

Marissa and Archie walk back towards Jack and I. She gives me an apologetic smile. "Sorry to steal him away, it's just the last time."

I try to smile. The guilt is only weighing on me more.

Suddenly, gunshots echo off the walls.

Everyone in the room starts panicking and starts to run out the back entrance.

They are getting louder, whoever is firing is coming inside. My first instinct is to reach in my purse and fight back. I'm not armed, and I haven't been for months. Archie shields me with his body, ready to take any bullet that comes near me.

Marissa looks like a ghost. The blood has completely washed away from her face.

Another gunshot gets fired, all four of us drop down hiding behind a table. *Like that's going to protect us.*

"Jack, get her out of here now." I look up at Archie and kiss him.

"I love you."

Martin found me. He wouldn't be firing on innocent people, even he has his limits. He's shooting at the Barker Cartel. I'm not going down without a fight.

Archie holds me against him. "Siren. You need to go."

I turn to look at Marissa who is still sitting beside Jack. "You need to go, now."

She runs away. The entire ballroom is empty except for us.

I poke my head around the other side of the table looking at Ron laying on the ground gasping for air. I turn back around grabbing Archie's hand. "Ron's down. I need a gun."

Archie's entire body goes stiff. His skin is suddenly frozen. "Hayley, who the fuck are you?"

I poke my head around the table again seeing Noah's large frame, Charles and Zack. Martin sent three of his followers that I have no relationship with and who aren't related to my friends Dad's. Three people who will not hesitate to shoot me.

I glance down at Ron, he has stopped moving and completely stopped gasping for air. He is only three feet away from me if that. I can get to him, I can get his gun.

"Hayley Cohen just fucking come out already. Your games are getting old." Noah is having fun, I can hear it in his voice and it is making me want to kill him even more.

"Cover me, I'll get Ron's gun then." I sneer.

"Bloody hell, Siren." Archie pulls out his gun slowly from the holster under his jacket. Any pieces he put together about me is coming crashing down on him now. "Don't make me regret this."

I snatch the gun from him, cocking it and I stand up tall. "It's Hayley Upton."

I try not to take my eyes off the targets, but members of the Cartel are laying dead on the floor. There are at least ten of them, all dead. A shiver shoots down my spine, but it's replaced with the murder that rushes through my veins. Charles raises his gun, I know he's fast so I pull the trigger firing the gun through his chest. Zack doesn't even have time to process what is happening before I shoot him in the arm, which he is using to hold his gun. Thankfully, he was out of bullets and it misses fire as his hand gave out causing it to crash onto the floor.

I point my gun at Noah, panting.

He puts his hands in the air. "Martin needs you to come back to New York."

"Put your gun down, Noah."

He does as he's told. I pass the gun back down to Archie.

Archie fly's up from the floor. "Who the fuck did I marry Hayley?"

I look back at Noah, he looks stunned. "I can't. I'm married."

Sirens sound off in the distance, all five of us run to the back entrance. We get outside watching the lights light up the darkness. Archie takes my hand, and we all follow him going the opposite way down an ally towards his car. The lights are coming up behind us fast, we all have no choice but to take off running. We are getting away and the sirens are becoming a faint noise in the background.

I stop, placing my hand on my hip, panting trying to breathe. "Did you have to shoot everyone?"

Zack turns around with pain spread across his face. "You bitch!"

Noah hits him across the head. "It's an exit wound you bitch. They saw our tattoos and they fired on us first, Cohen. You know the drill."

Archie raises his hand to his head. "You need to tell me everything now before I send you back to New York. I don't care if we are married. I'm fucking done being left in the dark. Ron is dead because of you. What tattoos? Why the fuck do you know how to shoot?"

"We need to call Alfie. Get him to meet us at your place." Jack is talking right through me, spitting out every single word in disgust. "Maybe he'll just bloody shoot her tonight."

I walk to Archie's car putting my head down.

***

I walk into the kitchen wetting a piece of paper towel scrubbing the cover-up from my arm. It was a bad idea, my arm is red and inflamed from the rubbing, and it's a reminder letting me know for the moment I'm still alive. I look down seeing the snake that destroyed my life. I light a smoke leaning against the countertop.

"You guys have been married for a week, half that time you never even spoke." Jack couldn't be making his feelings clearer.

"She knew who we were, and she wasn't scared. The PI I hired gave me my money back mate. I knew there was something going on." Archie responds I don't think they know I can hear them.

I can't even be mad or annoyed that he hired a PI. I gave him nothing to go off. I'm screwed up being okay with this. On the other hand, I told him I wanted to kill his dad, on our wedding day. I would want to know too.

I wipe my face as a tear fall down, I thought I knew what fear was. There is so much riding on me telling the truth.

"Arch," I call out, my voice is hardly loud enough to be heard.

He stands in front of me not looking at me.

"I need to go to New York. I don't have to come back. I just need you to sign the papers first." My hand begins to tremble at the thought of leaving him.

I want to crash onto the floor and cuddle in a ball, I can't imagine my life without him in it.

"Basilisk. I'm so stupid, those pictures, the snake." I look up to him and his face is drawn to my wrist. "Siren. Why didn't you tell me when I told you?"

"What did you expect me to say? Oh, hey me too. I'm on a hit list. You killed ten people, but I've killed fifty. I was running from my boss. I was just stupid enough to think he would never find me."

"Did your broth—"

"They never found me, they tried." I glance over to Noah, Archie closes his eyes slowly realising he almost blew their cover. "How am I supposed to tell you any of this?"

"I'm coming to New York with you. We are married, they can try to separate us, but they won't. Family is a big thing with the Basilisks, is it not?"

I take a puff, watching the cherry of the smoke burn. The entire world knows about the ruthless Mafia hiding away in New York City. We pretend like no one knows who we are. The Taylor family has had connections in every country for hundreds of years, even when a boss isn't from their bloodline, they still use those connections. We're a Mafia generated worldwide. I never covered up my tattoo every day to keep me from looking at it, I covered it, and so people didn't know who I was.

I nod. "As long as I corporate, Zack and Noah won't touch any of us. I can't ask you to come with me, Arch."

He wraps me in his arms. "You just told me you were on a hit list, Siren. I'm never letting you out of my sight again."

Chapter 19

Archie

Siren nuzzles her face in my chest. "Are we okay Arch? Can you ever forgive me for getting Ron killed? You don't have to stay with me out of obligation."

My words always come and nip me in the arse. I meant what I said, if she was honest with me, I could have prevented this. I knew something was wrong, I just never expected her to be a part of the bloody Basilisks. If I feel the weight on my shoulders with my death tally, I can't start to imagine how she is feeling. The nightmares, the dark paintings, I feel like a wanker. I know I love her, I'm just not sure if that's enough.

I'm not letting her go back to America alone. Even if I hate her right now, I'm not letting her be in any danger. I was scared to make her a Cartel wife when she already lived the worst life.

"Arch?" I can hear the begging in her voice.

I feel like I'm being pulled in multiple directions, my heart wants to forgive her. My mind is hating her more than I ever hated someone before. My grip has been loosening from her, I haven't even realised I'm not holding her anymore.

Siren is looking at me confused and hurt, she knows my answer. I don't even need to tell her.

I take a shaky breath, "I'm still coming with you, but I'm coming back alone."

My eyes are burning with hot tears, I need to man up. She's just a girl.

Hayley grabs on the counter, she is trying to hide her heartbreak. She's failing at it. Her hands are shaking, tears are falling down her face. "Archie, please don't do this."

I scrub my hands with my face. What am I doing? We both know I'm nothing without her, I can't walk away from her. I pull her back into my chest.

Her body is trembling trying to grab a hold of my shirt. "Please, Arch."

I close my eyes, this split decision changes both of our futures, if I walk away and she doesn't come back with me there's a good chance I never get to see her again.

I tangle my hands up in her hair. "You're coming back with me."

Siren starts to cry even more. She pushes herself away from me, wiping her face. "I wanted to tell you, it was too dangerous for you to know and I didn't want to add more onto you. We don't think about killing someone, you saw me tonight. I never wanted you to see that side of me, I thought if I could hide it."

I wipe her face with my thumb, how did this morning start so normal? "We need to go before Alfie gets here. Jack just stay low until we get back alright?" I raise my voice letting it be heard by everyone in the house.

"Alright, mate. Hayley, I'm pissed at you, really fucking pissed." He walks past me giving her a hug.

Hayley hugs him back whispering something to him then pulling away to grab my hand. "My closet is still full of clothes, go quickly pack. We don't have much time."

We arrive at London City airport. I'm thanking every god right now. The other two got seats on a plane that was departing when we arrived. I don't trust them. I don't trust any of them. Siren still hasn't told me what's going on, I want to trust her but even that is seeming to be difficult.

For all I know I am walking into my death trap completely unarmed. Me going with her was a stupid idea.

The TV in the corner is on mute, the subtitles are on. I want to pull my eyes away, I can't. I need to know what is going to happen when I come back. *The cameras were shot at, there is no footage of who did this. The police do know it was a conflict between the Baker Cartel and the Basilisks. Even with the attack at a public fundraiser, the public is in no harm.*

Hayley stands up and walks away leaving me alone in an airport waiting room. Even in the middle of the night, everyone is busy catching planes. People are sleeping in the chairs across from me. I hate flying, the thought of an aeroplane being able to stay in the sky because of 'aerodynamics' makes me nervous. I'm not going to tell her that until my feet are placed firmly on the ground back in London. I can do sixteen hours of flying both ways, as long as we don't hit turbulence, we stay clear of storms or we don't die in the ocean, I will be fucking good.

Hayley passes me a paper cup. "I got us goodnight tea, we can sleep on the plane. When we land everyone is just going to be waking up. Archie, I don't want you to fly back alone. You don't need to come."

"Why are you on the list Hayley?"

Her body tenses. "I ran away. I wanted something more, I needed to know who I was. I wanted to see the world."

I put my arm around her, bringing her close to my body. How am I supposed to stay mad at her when I know exactly how she's feeling? It wasn't in her intention to get Ron killed. People die in our lifestyles. I've held the hands of my dying friends more times than I can count. It never gets easier. That doesn't mean I need to forgive her. It also means I don't need to use it against her.

I kiss her hair looking up at the sign watching our flight slowly move to the top of the list. "I'm going to protect you. It doesn't mean I have forgiven you."

"Will you ever be able to?"

"I already am. I'm tired, physically and tired of our lives."

She cuddles up closer to me. "That's why I ran."

Just like that the hate I felt towards her is gone. I'm no longer mad at her.

I understand.

Chapter 20

Hayley

Sleeping on a plane is the most uncomfortable position I have ever forced my body into. We somehow managed to stay asleep for the entire eight hours. Archie is acting like everything is okay, how the hell can this be okay? His best friend is dead because of me. Jack is hiding low, staying clear of Alfie. I caused so many issues, I'm the reason why ten more people are dead. It wasn't me that pulled the trigger, it makes no fucking difference. My death toll spiralled to sixty-one and one of those was a Basilisk.

"You need to change before Martin sees you in those sweats."

I spin around, the sun is poking out over the building of the airport. My eyes are taking long enough to adjust. Dillon's voice is making every muscle in my body want to give out. It isn't being in New York that's doing it to me, it's being in his beautiful presence. I haven't spoken to him since he called me drunk. He looks at me like I'm his big sister and I look at him as if he is my little brother. He is close with William and Liam, they weren't the one who he came out to, I was.

I will never forget the fear in his eyes when he told me he was gay, I never had to ask him to repeat it, it was written all over his face. I never cared; he is who he is. Everyone in our group just looked at him, acknowledged it and moved on with their day until they realised why he was so scared. Martin doesn't do well with change. Since Dillon is a Taylor he has a chance of moving on as boss.

We all sat in the room while he told Martin, it ended up not being a big deal. Martin is a shitty person. This was really the only thing Martin ever acted as a father on and not a Mob boss. The Basilisks are meant to have families to keep the bloodlines going, no adoption agency would be stupid enough to hand one of us a child. That's why Liam is so hell bound on getting married and having kids to save me.

I drop Archie's hand running up to Dillon trying not to break down in tears, again. I have a lot of reunions to do today before Martin makes his decision on me. "Dilly."

He sets me to the ground glaring at me. "You know I hate that nickname." He looks past me and smiles.

I bat his arm knowing what he's thinking.

Archie shakes his hand. "I'm assuming your Dillon? Let's get my wife changed and deal with this."

Dillon pulls back his hand picking up my suitcase. "Liam is going to shit himself, Hayley. Have you talked to Spencer?"

I shake my head.

"Cameron was supposed to meet him at the Statue of Liberty. He was going to propose, and she blew him off. He's been trying to stalk her. She's completely taken off. We also have a funeral to attend tomorrow. Sammy shot someone, a random person. Martin paid off the family as condolences."

Archie takes my hand. "Should we really be talking about this here?"

"Everyone knows who we are. They also know we won't hurt random people."

"Apparently not," Archie mutters, I can't blame him for being upset right now.

I get in the back seat of the car giving Archie the passenger seat for him and Dillon to get to know each other. The city looks the same as I left it. When I was homesick, I wasn't missing my home, I was missing the people who made it home. Getting away was everything I ever needed, and here I am back in the hell I ran from. Through my gaze from the window, I can hear the guys laughing. Archie knows who they are, but they have no idea who Archie is.

I should have told them, at least William, Spencer and Josh they know everything I thought was going on. I never filled them in on the rest. I'm lying to everyone about so much, I don't even know what the fucking truth is anymore. My mind is being pulled in every possible direction.

I move over to the middle seat in the back placing my hand on Archie's shoulder. He is probably terrified right now. "Arch."

He reaches up on his shoulder grabbing my hand. "Siren, don't bloody apologise for one more time okay? I need a gun. I'm not going in there unarmed."

Dillon turns into the parking lot of my apartment. "You can have mine. Do we need you to teach you how to shoot it?"

Archie snorts. "No Mate. I'll be alright. Any more secrets you're keeping, Siren?"

I take my hand back from Archie's shoulder moving back over to my original seat, he doesn't sound mad at me one bit. Dillon is staring at me in the rear-view mirror confused as hell.

I open the door. "Explain everything to him please."

I shut the door walking away, if I have to talk about how eleven people died because of me, I'm going to be a weeping mess. Hopefully, Noah and Zack fill everyone in by the time I get to Martins so I can stop reliving this. Charles body likely isn't coming back to America, that's on me. I can't run away from this. Whatever Martin does to me I deserve.

My apartment and I go back since I was sixteen and kicked out of my sperm donor's house. The father who raised me disowned me when I was fourteen when he found out I wasn't his. That's another secret I'm keeping from Archie. I need to give up my lease on my apartment, it's just so hard to do. This is where I lived while in high school, this was my home for four years. I take a deep breath opening the door, everything is still in the same order as I left it, only with a layer of dust on everything. I had enough money to buy a house out right years ago, I couldn't say goodbye to my one bedroom.

The walls are painted white, the television is sitting on the TV stand. My entire wall in the living room is plastered with photos of the seven of us. I even have a few from before Erik lost his trust in me. People who would look at these without really knowing us would say we are annoying with how close we are. They aren't wrong, other than Erik I am the only one who lives alone, and he owns a house right down the road from Adam. There's a difference from what they see though, we survive off each other. If one person falls, we all do.

We are the family that's held each other up, we all raised each other. Our parents did none of it. Our moms tried, they were distracted. All of us were bred to be the next generation of Basilisk, other than me. I was a complete mistake from an affair. That doesn't matter though, being a Basilisks is in my blood.

I walk down the hallway to my bedroom. I need to find a dress. I need to do my makeup and do something with my hair so I can fit back in with the code of always looking my best and always being in uniform.

What feels like hours later I am dressed in a black low cut short dress, my hair is curled and my makeup is done to the ultimate level of perfection like it used to be. I'm pouring a cup of whiskey, I need something to give me the courage to face today and if it just happens that I need a lot of liquid courage, then so be it. I tip my head back feeling like I'm drowning in half a cup of whiskey. I slam the cup on the counter and walk out of my apartment.

I get down the stairs to see Archie and Dillon both in the car still alive. I try to walk in a straight line, but I'm becoming lightheaded.

I open the car door and Dillon turns around fast. "A Cartel really Hayley?"

I move my hand up in the air pointing between me and Dillon. "Between the weapon smuggling and our death counts, we are worse than he ever will be." The strong smell of whisky is lingering in the car.

Archie turns around in his seat. "Siren, I know you're scared. It's only ten relax on the alcohol."

I place my hands on his cheeks. "How are you not scared?"

"I've been losing my mind since I saw you shoot my gun. I'm happy I can finally understand you a little bit better."

I lean in to kiss Archie, he pulls away buckling up his seat belt.

"He's so much better for you." Dillon glances up in the rear-view mirror flashing me his billion-dollar Taylor smile.

Chapter 21

Hayley

The three of us walk into Martin's dining room. The large table is making me sick to my stomach remembering all the awkward family get-togethers. Thanksgiving and Christmas got so bad and so tense between me and my 'fathers' that Kinsley started to refuse to do Thanksgiving. Liam watches me walk in and every muscle in his body freezes, it pains me to see how much love he has for me that I can't return. Spencer looks like he's a completely different person. I want to find Cameron and strangle her for hurting my brother like this. The pain in his eyes, she has changed him.

Adam jogs up to me, scooping me off my feet into a hug. "You're a bitch for leaving."

"I love you too, Adam." He sets me on the ground, I walk backwards searching for Archie's hand. "This is him." I look stupid from the huge smile on my face, my cheeks are already starting to hurt.

Liam runs up to me, his grey eyes are piercing my soul. He grabs my hand pulling me into the Kitchen. Before we get through the swinging doors, I look over my shoulder to see Archie glaring at Liam. Josh pats him on the shoulder, his body doesn't loosen up.

Liam turns around placing his hand under my chin making me look up at him. He's about to kiss me, this is what he does before he kisses me. His forehead touches mine and his nose rests beside mine.

I take a deep breath. "I'm married."

He places his hand on my back, trying to pull me closer. "It's not like you love him. I love you, Hayley."

I push him off me, he tries to fight. Suddenly his face drops. "I love him."

I thought I would see him angry, not hurt. Liam walks backwards not taking his eyes from me. "You are supposed to marry me." He isn't asking me a question, he's trying to process it. "I haven't found the right girl. She has to be here somewhere. I'll find her, I'll ask her to marry me. I can save all of us. Then we can be together."

His plan makes him sound like a psychopath. None of it makes any sense. He never even heard me when I told him I love Archie. "Liam, I don't love you. Not like I used to."

He stomps up to me, kissing me fiercely. "I'm not giving up on you."

I raise my hand to my hair letting out a sob. My heart is pounding in my chest, Archie is going to lose his mind, adding that on top of everything I put him through. I look over, nearly jumping out of my skin, my husband watched another man kiss me.

I'm trying to breathe. It feels like I'm hyperventilating. I never pushed him away, I never saw him coming. "I'm so sorry."

Archie takes a step towards me reaching his hands out to welcome me into his body. "You guys were screaming at each other. The entire house heard you."

I never even realised we were raising our voices. We are poison to one another. Being each other's right-hand man had brought us together, the fighting only brought on makeup sex. As soon as the fighting ended the sex started. I thought that was what love was supposed to be like, I don't anymore. Not since I fell in love with Archie. I let go of my toxic relationship with Liam, he has yet to do the same with me. He needs to be cut free from the Basilisk, only then will he be able to let go of me.

"Martin knows I'm here then. I need to go, Archie."

He nods then brings his lips down to kiss me. "When you get out you need to explain to me why your brothers look nothing alike. I'll try not to knock Liam on his ass."

I smile slightly breathing out my nose. I take his hand walking back out the swinging doors walking to Martin's office. Archie and I let go of each other's hands. I don't look back, I can't bring myself to look back. Everyone is talking about the future like I have one. This might very well be the end of me, I am walking into my death trap.

I shut the large doors behind me, Martin stands up pointing his gun pressing on the trigger. I drop my head letting out a sigh, he just tried Russian roulette. He does it again and my heart is pounding in my chest.

Nothing.

"Come here now." Martin empties his gun on the desk.

I walk over, already knowing my name is engraved on a bullet. I only have one power over him right now and I'm hoping to hell that's enough. "I'm married."

He sits down glaring at me, pushing the bottom of his jaw out. "You killed one of my men."

"Sammy killed an innocent person." Okay, maybe I have two things over him.

He tosses me the bullet with my name engraved with a small snake on it. "I've never had to make one of those for a Basilisk before. I can use you in London, I need someone to organise the weapons sales over there, get them on ships and get them here. Someone I *trust* will be transporting them. You just need to show up to the sales with whomever I send for pickup. Since you killed Charles, I am down a weapons dealer here."

"I'm married to the soon to be Baker Cartel boss." I squeeze the bullet in my hand reassuring myself that It's still safely in my grasp.

"Get the fuck out of my office before I make sure my guns are fully loaded."

I nod not sticking around long enough for him to repeat himself. I'm still alive, even though I'm still a basilisk I'm not taking any of my time for granted. I open the doors, no one took their eyes off the door. I toss the bullet to Josh, watching Spencer's broken eyes get wide as it lands in my brothers' hands.

"Russian roulette will make your heart stop. Wouldn't recommend it." My voice is a lot lighter and cheerful than it should be. I walk over to Archie wrapping my arm around him, forcing him into me. "You marrying me saved my life, just like I thought it would."

He pulls me into his chest taking a deep breath. "I'll be the only person you ever marry."

"Oh! Shots fired!" William slammed his hands on the table looking nothing less than amused.

"Fuck every single one of you." Liam mumbles.

***

I run my hands over the table glancing up at Archie. "Seriously Spence? You come here every single day waiting for her to come to work?"

"I don't wait here for hours. Jesus, I'm not *that* creepy. It makes no sense for her to just leave like this. She didn't have to ghost me and quit her job to make her point across."

"You need to get your mind off her mate." Archie pokes at his fries. "Now I understand why you felt so weird calling those chips. It's like we're on another plant."

Spencer leans forward placing his elbows on the table holding his head, "I need to sleep around."

Archie sighs, taking me off guard. "I didn't say that, but sure."

I steal food from Archie's plate ignoring the sour look on his face. "Keep her ring, you are going to regret it if you get rid of it, Spence."

Archie looks around White rock. "Why are all the tables around us clear and everyone's staring at us?"

"This is what being a Basilisk is like. These assholes always make girls stop and stare."

Archie shrugs his shoulders clearly uncomfortable with the attention, he doesn't even realise how much the attention is drawn on him. It's heart-breaking to see Spencer like this, he is normally the happiest one out of all of us. We are used to waves of emotions, but this isn't coming in waves for him. He is stuck in this depressing state. I wish I could get in his mind, find out if she was upset with him. They had the relationship you dream of growing up, the one that you know is impossible to find, but you never stop searching for it.

She would stay up until the early hours of the morning to make sure he was alive after he got called away, Spencer was Cameron's rock as much as she was his. At least I thought. I never saw them together, it was the way he talked about her. I guess everything was one-sided. We love harder, we fight harder, because everything could be taken away from us faster than we can blink. You don't understand it unless you are like us, maybe that was what went wrong.

Spencer finally picks up his burger. "Liam's lost his mind. Martins sent us on a mission to replace Charles, so thanks for that. Does he really think getting married will be enough?"

Archie's body tenses. "Almost as much as kissing Siren will get her back."

"How did you not knock him out?" Spencer grins. "I would have. Thanks for taking care of her man."

Archie sinks into his seat. Now, it's my turn to fill someone in on everything that is happening in London. Spencer will nod, glare at Archie or just stare off into space every few seconds. The gears behind his eyes are working and the anger is rushing to his face. I was hoping Dillon would do it for me, he's probably telling everyone right now. Reliving it feels like a dream, everything we are going back to doesn't feel real.

The table is quiet, Archie grabs my hand. We are both staring at Spencer waiting for him to process the news. He isn't normally like this. His heart being shattered is taking a toll on him.

"You still went through with the sham marriage even though it wasn't a sham, to protect Hayley, even though it was going to destroy your life?"

Maybe he wasn't processing the news but trying to make more sense of it than I can.

"I liked you before, now I'm proud to call you my brother-in-law."

Spencer leans back in his seat, his amber eyes radiating. Our lives are so screwed up, my story was less than comforting, and that doesn't change the fact that Archie has saved my life. I really didn't think getting married was going to stop Martin from killing me, I knew it would keep me away from him. If I was single, he would have tried to fire his gun once or twice, even until the entire clip was to be empty just in case there was a chance, I was still alive. Love is the only weakness he has and that is because of Kinsley, somehow she loves him even though he is the definition of what a real-life monster is.

I look up to Spencer batting his eyes at a girl who is shorter than I am, but still tall. Her brown hair is tied up in a ponytail and she is thin. If guys have a standard of beautiful this chick is it. Her face has grief written all over it. Her eyes are red and puffy, I want to hold her. I don't even know her, and my heart is breaking for her.

"Hi, Spence." She is really good at covering everything up, only a person with a motherly love towards others can hear it.

"Has anyone told you how beautiful you are?"

"Just you, for the last three days."

I cover my mouth trying to hide a laugh. She sounds so annoyed, it's hilarious. Watching the guys strike out is one of my favourite things. It never happens, when it does, they are usually a lesbian and start to hit on me. She looks smarter than the other girls that have come in their path.

"Lizzy, don't be like that."

She rolls her eyes and walks away. *I love her.*

Spencer leans in ignoring the delight written all over my face. "I'm going to conquer her, just wait and see."

Archie leans in close to him. "Three hundred says you won't."

"You're on."

They never spoke in London, which never once made me think I made a bad decision with Archie. I knew everyone would get along. I just didn't think they would get along this well. I don't understand mine and Archie's relationship, I don't understand why he would marry me knowing what is in store for him. I don't know if I ever will fully understand it, I'm not going to be able to ever stop blaming myself either. In less than a week, he is going to be in charge of the Baker Cartel and there's nothing I can do about it.

Chapter 22

Hayley

Sitting in a room full of my other halves is the best feeling in the world. I was right, Dillon filled everyone in on everything. We walked into Spencer's house to Josh giving Archie the biggest man hug I've ever witnessed in my life. Even Liam has seemed to back off a little bit. He looks more hurt than I've ever thought possible, he's trying. He won't be trying forever, hopefully, if he does act out on his plan he may actually fall in love. Maybe she will be as beautiful and as incredible as he really does deserve. I have no idea who she is, but I feel for her already.

Everyone is going to want to tell her the truth, Liam might even trick everyone and make them think he has fallen in love with her. She may never know until I tell her. If she finds out on her own then that would be great, who's going to believe the girl with a British accent who just walks in and owns the place? I sure as hell wouldn't.

"Whiskey?" Adam looks at Archie.

"Anything less intense? Siren buy's limes for tequila."

"She doesn't use limes."

"They were for me."

Laughter erupts. Archie isn't even embarrassed. He follows Adam into the kitchen, glancing over his shoulder at me. I thought he would back off calling me Siren when he was around people, I'm not going to lie. I love how he still does it. No one bats an eye at it either.

William sits down beside me putting his arm over my shoulder. I lay my head on him falling into relaxation. We really should be closer than we are. His Mother died as collateral damage when he was younger, his father died from being shot a few years later. He is the only one other than Josh that knows what it feels like to lose your mom. I guess, I kind of resent him. He knows where his mothers' body is. I'm the reason we aren't as close as we should be. That doesn't stop him from trying.

"If you ever need us for anything, you need to let us know. We just don't like the thought of you being an unarmed Basilisk." William rubs my shoulder with his hand as he talks.

"She won't be." Archie walks out from the kitchen with a beer in his hand passing me a glass of whiskey. "My dad bought weapons from Martin a while ago. She would have one by now, but she never told me who she was."

"I hate how I like you." Liam whips Archie his smoke pack. "I don't regret kissing her, I never will and if you hurt her, I will fly to London and decapitate you without a second thought."

Archie lights the smoke between his lips exhaling. "I thought the threat was going to be worse."

Liam smirks. I look over at Josh and he smiles, shaking his head. Archie has won everyone over. I don't know how he has done it. Liam is the hardest person to get through and somewhere between his actions and his words he knocked down the wall. He's knocked down every wall that my brothers put up for them to protect me. Most of all, he's knocked down every wall I built, he makes me feel like there is something good buried down under my darkness. He found the good in me before I ever did.

This is what love is. Love isn't fighting every day because you are both strung out on your lifestyle. Love should be able to pull you out of it, let you remind you that you are better than you see yourself as. That's what Archie does for me.

I haven't done a single thing in my life to deserve this. I'm happy as hell I found it.

***

Archie sits on my pink velvet couch. It is the most uncomfortable piece of furniture that I own, it is just so beautiful I had to buy it. He is eyeing up the rustic end tables and coffee table surrounding the couch and the matching TV stand. His eyes land on all the photos covering the walls.

He turns to me. "If I wasn't so comfortable, I would be furious about half of those pictures."

I close my eyes, I never saw a point in taking down the pictures of me and Liam. The way he looks at me in them says exactly how much he loves me. I never thought I would be in a relationship again. I want to take them down right now, it's hard. He was my first love and even though our relationship wasn't the best, he is still my best friend. I can't just change my memories because I moved on.

Archie looks around the room. "Let's move your things into our house."

I look at him with a smile starting to spread across my face. I've been smiling so much today, my face hurts.

"We will pack everything you want. We can just leave someone in charge of meeting the movers."

I land on the couch beside Archie kissing him. I've been tiptoeing around the house, the art room makes it feel like it's mine. Not having any of my things there just reminds me it isn't my home, not really. I turn the TV on, I never cancelled my television. I never thought I was going to be in London as I have been.

"Tell me about your family, Siren." Archie's voice is stern.

I lean back. "Josh and I have the same mom. My mom cheated on Josh's dad with Spencer's dad. Apparently, they were in love with each other. My mother led Josh's dad to believe I was his kid. As I got older, I started to look less like Josh and a lot more like Spencer. Everyone was asking questions. It was clear my dad wasn't who she said was."

"After I was born, Spencer's dad pulled away from his wife. Once the truth was out everything went to shit. My mom went missing, but when you are dealing with the Basilisks, if you go missing, you're dead. Josh's dad kicked me out of the house. Spencer's dad let me move in with them. As soon as I turned sixteen both his parents kicked me out. Then I rented this place."

"What does everything think happened to your mom?"

"No one knows Arch. I have my theories. Josh has blocked out her existence like we normally do when someone dies. Spencer won't listen to it because he won't admit it might be true. I think Spencer's mom killed my mom. Being married to a Basilisk and hearing what we do can change a person, I think she got sucked in trying to protect her family. She let me move in because it wasn't my fault I was born, she never looked at me for two years. I stayed out of her way."

"Do you have your mom's eyes?"

I smile, my eyes are always everyone's favourite feature. "Yes. It made living with Spencer's family so much harder. His dad would look at me and see his daughter she left behind, and his mom would see the eyes from the women she may have killed."

With a deep breath, all the weight that was on my chest has been lifted off of me. Archie finally knows who I am inside and out. There aren't any more lies, or untold secrets burning from my past inside of me. It feels like I just grew wings. I didn't realize how much the lying was weighing me down.

"Mrs. Upton, I promise you if we ever have kids we will give them the perfect home. We can even keep them away from our jobs."

I scrunch my nose. "A gangster and a Cartel having kids? That's a recipe for a hurricane."

"No kids then?"

"No, I don't think so. It's not that I don't love you. If I'm ever given the chance I want to travel."

Archie lowers his head. I never thought about discussing this before we got married. Sure, I was planning on him falling for me. I never thought we would be having this discussion because I never wanted kids, it never crossed my mind.

"Thank fucking Christ." He looks back up at me smiling. "We can just be the kick-ass aunt and uncles."

My heart nearly stops. "You're not mad?"

"I'm so relieved. Even if we did get out of this shit, I still wouldn't be able to do it. As long as we can be together, I'll be better than alright."

I lay on the couch resting my head on my husband's lap. He is full of surprises today, I never knew it was possible to fall in love with someone all over again, but I am. He has stripped my soul down to the last lair and still loves me with all of his heart. For the first time in my life, I am looking forward to my future.

Chapter 23

Hayley

We are standing so far back from the family. All of the Basilisks who are based in New York are here standing on the side-lines for the girl who was shot and killed by Sammy. We can't hear anything, we can't see her picture. We don't need to, we need to stand here in black silently apologising for her life-ending.

The cries from her family are going to haunt me until the day I die. Funerals are nothing new to me, but this one is. This one is the reason why all nine of us are standing here hating our lives. Archie puts his arm around me pulling me into his chest. We weren't even on American soil when she was killed, it doesn't make a difference.

"There's a lot of people from school here," Adam whispers.

We all look around. Right away I recognise every face that I can see. I want to see the seven people that are kneeling down at the grave crying harder than I ever thought it was possible to cry. Maybe then the big secret Martin is hiding about who it was would be out in the open.

"Erik, do you know who it is?" Spencer asks, he runs his hands through his hair panicking.

"Man, it's not her. I swear to you, I checked with my captain." Erik says calmly.

All of us let out a shaky breath, we are strong but that would break Spencer. Then it would break all of us. We wouldn't be able to ignore her death like everyone else.

I look around the crowd of Basilisks trying to find Sammy, I see his sister Violet, but he isn't there. How could he be so stupid? He was the getaway driver, completely unnecessary to shoot. I wish we could hear them. I just want to know her name.

"I need to go. I can't stand here." Dillon starts to back away. "This is what we do you guys, we destroy people."

None of us argues, we all walk away behind Dillon. The grief and the cries are too much for any of our mental states. Archie reaches down to my hand. I can't stand the thought of him blaming me for Ron. I can't go back to the fear that overtook my body in our Kitchen. I don't want him to come up twenty years from now and Archie reminds me that he's dead because of me.

He is dead because of me. I wasn't expecting to move and suddenly have eleven more lives hanging above my head.

I lean into Archie squeezing his hand, the words I thought I was thinking start to leave my tongue. "I caused eleven funerals."

Archie stops turning me around placing his hands on my cheeks. "You never caused their deaths. It comes with the job, you hear me?"

I wrap my arms around Archie letting him hold me. He doesn't blame me, I blame myself. I hate myself. I should have never been so stupid. Once I found out, I should have said something. Alfie is going to have my head when we get back.

We both step away from each other's embrace. Both of my 'fathers' are staring at me, they are standing side by side. Somehow they have managed to kick me out of their lives but stayed friends, even though they both love or loved the same women, knowing she returned her feelings to both of them.

Archie follows my glare putting the pieces together almost immediately, he grabs my hand ploughing through them. "You're missing out, she's pretty great."

I have to fight back a sob from shock. I wasn't expecting him to say anything to them. The grip from his hand is tightening making me realise how mad he really is. He loosens his grip; ever since he grabbed my wrist he's been extra careful not to hurt me. Other than slamming me against the wall when Marissa barged in, now that I know what was happening, I get it. I understand all of it. That makes me look bad, I'm fully aware of it.

I pull a smoke out of my purse handing Archie the pack. "I need to go see April before we leave."

Josh looks at me frowning. "We just got you back here though."

"We have some pretty serious shit to deal with, are you coming with me to see her?"

Dillon, William and Liam all grunt at the same time.

I turn to look at them. "Get over it."

"She's such a bitch, Josh can do better. So much better." William mumbles getting into the driver side of his car.

Josh turns around holding his fist to his side hopping in the passenger's side of Spencer's car. Adam sits beside me, and Archie is on the other side of me in the back seat. I'm only here for a few more hours and I feel the weight hanging down on everyone. Everything we are getting moved to London is in boxes, I called movers and the guys already volunteered to donate the rest of the apartment for me. More than anything, I wish I could stay so I could be with them. I made the choice to leave and now I have to deal with it.

I get out of the car running inside of Willys towards the bar. I spot April looking more beautiful than ever, even in her mid-twenties, she looks so sophisticated. Her family thinks she's a bitch, but that's only because she wants them to believe she is. William and now Liam have been using her to get with her friends, she said enough was enough and started to bite back about fifty times harder than it was necessary. She doesn't want to see me, I know that. The only difference is I don't care, she is stuck with me because of her off and on relationship with Josh. They wouldn't be so off and on if it wasn't for her family.

She turns around and to my surprise, she smiles and runs up to me hugging me. "Good god! Woman. I never thought I would see you again." She pulls away looking at Archie from his feet to his head. "Is this him?"

Liam walks past. "The one who stole my girl? Yeah, that's him."

"Fuck off Liam." April sneers. "I don't like good people dating my good for nothing brother."

Archie walks away with Adam while talking to April. "Don't let her drink anything, we have a flight."

Josh glares at April watching her knees give out from his accent. This is what I missed, April and I were never close, none of that matters. She's clearly willing to move on and I was ready years ago. I need to enjoy the last little bit of time

that I have with everyone. I need to have a goodbye and say
that I love them, because the truth is, I may have gotten myself
off one hit list, but I may have added my name on another one.

Chapter 24

Archie

I sit up in bed watching my beautiful wife sleep. Seeing her fall apart from saying goodbye was the hardest thing I ever had to witness. She sobbed almost the entire flight to London until she fell asleep on my shoulder. I think half those tears were her leaving and the other half scared for her life about coming back here. If Alfie wants her dead, he is going to have to go through me first. I'm really hoping he hesitates to pull the trigger.

My phone buzzes. *Let me in, mate.*

I fly out of bed, tossing on the first pair of sweatpants I see. I run down the stairs sliding a shirt over my head.

I open the door letting Jack slide in, closing it and locking it behind him.

"Where is she? Did, did Hayley come back?" He rubs his hands on his pant legs. "Bloody hell mate, please tell me she came back."

"She's asleep in our bed. Her boss set her up as a weapons dealer here in the city." I watch Jack close his eyes exhaling hard, it looks like a wave of relief just crashed into him. "You regret saying you want her dead? Bloody knob head. She is going to need a friend by the end of the day, you better have a fucking good apology."

I walk away sitting on the couch lighting a fag. He doesn't need an apology. I don't think his words have even crossed Siren's mind since we left. She understands everything all too well. I'm going to make him apologise, out of respect for my wife. She needs someone other than me to fall back on, and he is the only person other than Jason who she spends any of her time with and even then, only one out of those two people know who she really is.

Jack sits down and the next thing I know I am gossiping like a teenage girl. Everything that happened in New York is coming out of my mouth all in one breath. "Other than Liam kissing her, I actually like him, and it makes me bloody furious. The Basilisks have two cops on their side, one of them is her friend's brother."

Jack's face scrunches up and he shakes his head once, "How do they get away with that?"

"I don't think they do. Martin and everyone else are so hell bound on not getting caught, they are sloppy with it."

"Two days at a five-star hotel with room service is a bloody paradise." Jack kicks his feet up on the coffee table leaning back on the couch.

"Glad you had a good time," I mumble under my breath. "Let's go game."

***

"Siren, wake up." I open the bedroom door. We have been gaming for hours and it's well into the afternoon.

182

I walk to the bedroom and panic strikes my body. The bed is completely empty, the sheets are a mess.

"Siren!" I scream my heart is beating so loud in my ears I can't hear anything then the pulse and the blood rush to my head. "Where the fuck are you?"

I run down the stairs checking the living room and kitchen. I've been home this entire time. I should have heard her wake up. Jack should have heard her.

"Mate what are you yelling about?" Jack runs downstairs behind me.

"She's fucking gone. We were here." I raise my hands to the back of my neck, interlocking my fingers, letting the truth settle in my mind. "Dad must have been watching the house. What did you do?"

"Bloody hell, I did nothing."

I scrub the face with my hands, I had to ask him even though I know he is on our side. I need her back. I failed her. I promised her and everyone else I would keep her safe and she was taken from our house.

My mum has a bloody key. She could have let her guard down for half a second, trusting Alfie and he would have taken it.

Jack is making phone calls. I can't hear anything he is saying. My mind is stuck in panic mode. Desperate to get the women of my dreams back.

Hayley

My head is pounding, and my neck is being supported by my shoulder with an intense pain radiating through it. My eyes are still closed, but I can see the bright lines shining through my eyelids. The air is musty, I think it's mould.

I know I'm not at home in the safety of Archie's arms. If I open my eyes the Bakers are going to know I'm awake. I can't move until they force me awake.

Four years of being a Basilisk I have never been put in this position, I've never even thought about this hypothetically, even though I chose not to think about it, here I am. Away from my husband, I want to believe he had no idea this was happening, but he was home. He should have been home to stop this.

I'm going to die, I'm the only Basilisk in London, and no one knows I'm here. My mind is taking me back to Josh, Spencer, Dillon, William, Liam, and Adam, smiling, happy. I'm even thinking about Erik. I'm imagining being wrapped up in Archie's arms one last time feeling the warmth of his body, even if he is the reason I'm here. A single tear rolls down my cheek.

I jumped when a hand wipes away my tears. My ankles are tied to the legs of the chair and my arms are tied behind my back.

"I'm going to get you and my son out of this." I'm not sure if I'm hallucinating Olivia's soft voice or if she is really here. "Jacks calling him, love, don't give up."

Her body leaves my side, she is really here. Why is she here?

I slowly open my eyes, I'm alone in this huge room. The sun is shining in from the broken windows on top of the building. Metal stairs with a metal railing are circulating around the building with doors open wide. This is an old warehouse. The longer I sit here the smell of mould is only becoming more and more intense. I can hear traffic from outside, London is still moving, the citizens are living their lives completely unaware that I'm going to die. My neck is so stiff, I don't want to move it from my shoulder, I don't know how long I've been here for.

I want to pray. I just don't know who or what would listen to me other than Satan himself. I want to ask for everyone I love to find happiness, to be set free from this hell. I want the family of the girl that the Basilisks killed to find peace, I want the grieving girl from the restaurant to be okay. I want another bloody chance at life. I want to know what real freedom means.

Alfie's voice travels into the room. "Start with cutting off her tattoo. We can't have the trace of another dead Basilisk in London."

I swallow hard fighting against the itchy rope on my arm. I'm pulling and fighting as hard as I can, I can't win against the knot.

"Good, you're awake. Good for us, not you. We get to watch you suffer." He's smiling, the sick bastard is enjoying himself.

Alfie pulls up a chair with the back of it facing me, he sits down with his arms on the back leaning into it.

Scanning the four men standing behind Alfie they all look like amateurs compared to the basilisk men, it only means they are smarter. I'm out of my league. There is no chance of me getting out alive, even with Olivia here, I'm fucked, I'm going to die, and they are going to be smiling while they kill me.

I never thought I would feel so ashamed of the actions I have taken in life, I thought I was saving myself by running. I had no idea this was going to happen. I got myself killed, but I don't regret it for a second. I found Archie. I know what real love is because of him. I sound cheesy, pathetic even. Every second with him was worth it. Even though it started as a 'friend date', it ended as something so much more than that.

They can take everything else away from me, but they can't take that from me.

Alfie nods his head towards me. "Untie her and hold her down."

It's been six years since my mom died and I want to call out for her, I want to scream out to my fathers to finally have them protect me.

The rope is untied and there is more pressure than needed from the three men pushing me down onto the chair to stop me from moving. I'm trapped, I can't even move my arm to try and stop him.

"Siren, I'm here baby," Archie's voice is low but reassuring.

Alfie raises his gun to my head with the steadiest hand I've ever seen, the men drop their hands from me, backing away, and he pulls the trigger.

I drop my head letting out a deep breath, it's Russian roulette all over again.

I raise my head again staring straight in the barrel. Archie's and Jack's voices are echoing. His hand is on the trigger, suddenly a gunshot is fired.

Archie

My legs are shaking, my heart is pounding in my chest and tears have made their way down my face. My dad falls over with blood spewing out from the back of his head, the bullet went right through soaking Siren in his blood.

She opens her eyes, frozen. She isn't breathing, but she's fucking alive. "Olivia." She takes a sharp breath.

I run over to my wife fighting with the rope on her ankles. "I'm so sorry. I fucked up. I thought you were home. I shouldn't have left your side." I look at her tattoo, the knife never even got a chance to cut her skin. Other than the trauma, she is completely unharmed. "I love you."

"Archie, your mom."

I turn to look where his eyes are locked on. My mum is standing with a gun in her hands, her entire body is shaking. Jack slowly takes the gun from her sliding it across the floor. Her face is completely white. Sirens are floating in through the broken windows. I turn back around fighting with the ropes.

As soon as the footsteps get closer to us, I drop the rope from Siren's shaking legs and cover her with my sweater, covering the tattoo from the police. I pull her into me, holding her. She holds my body as tight as she can like she is saying goodbye.

My mum has her hands behind her head, staring at me. "I called you. My husband was trying to bring my son, his friend and his wife into this life, so I killed him."

Jack and I look at each other with the same confused expression, this was my stupid plan.

I hold my wife closer to me, watching the police arrest my mum. She's talking to them and others are walking to the other four of Alfie's followers, arresting them too.

A police officer walks up to us watching Siren. "Do you need to go to the hospital, Mrs Upton?"

Her body relaxes against mine. He's American, his accent hasn't even started to come out yet.

I look down at Siren, she shakes her head. "I just want to go home, can we go home?"

She's trying to ask if I'm being arrested without actually asking if I'm arrested.

The cop nods. "Go home."

I look down on his name tag reading *Brooks.*

***

I shut the television off, it's all over the news. With Mum killing Alfie and the police involvement in the investigation the Baker Cartel is done, over. I'm free. Jack is sitting on the couch next to me fagging more than he should be. We all are. The house is a haze of smoke.

Siren grabs my hand. "Are you okay?"

I know that's a normal question to ask, but it suddenly makes me infuriated. Of course, I'm not okay, my mother was just arrested for murder when I should have been the one to pull the trigger.

"He's a Basilisk, I don't know how Martin got him here. I frankly don't want to know, but I'm almost wondering if that's how he found me."

"What the bloody hell are you talking about?" Jack exhales his smoke.

"The cop. The one who told us to go home. He's a bloody Basilisk."

I laugh, one that's far from humour. Two days ago, Hayley was on a hit list, and now Martin is protecting her.

Is it bad of me to be happy that I'm free even though Mum is going to be in jail for likely the rest of her life? She married Alfie not knowing the truth and now she is paying for it as a life jail sentence. She didn't do it for me to be crushed, she would probably smack me if she knew I was anything less than happy right now.

I take a deep breath. "We're free Jack."

Jack raises his beer in the air. "This one's for you, Ron."

I pull Siren into my chest kissing her head. For the first time in my life, I can taste the future.

Epilogue

Hayley

"No, Archie. What the bloody hell are you doing?" I facepalm, watching him landscape the backyard is a mix of emotions. Mostly him making me mad and then laughing.

He drops a brick on the ground. "This would be easier if you would stop criticizing me!" He smiles. "Have I ever told you I miss you sounding like an American?"

He rushes up to me picking my feet off the ground layering me in kisses. He has been an entirely new person in the last few months since he has been free from the Cartel, he wakes up every single morning happy and excited to start the day. That includes making fun of my art degree. Life with Archie is already better than I ever thought it could be.

I only have one or two deliveries a month for Martin. I haven't fired a gun since the ball and my nightmares have completely stopped. Life is good, life is easy.

"Marry me again," Archie pulls away, rubbing my cheek with his palm. "Let's do it in New York. You can meet Charlie and Lizzy. We can do it when Brittney's back."

The day Spencer called me to tell me that Cameron's real name was Brittney, and she was recruited to the FBI to save him made my heart stop. I still have mixed emotions about being at her fake funeral. I never heard my brother cry in my life, but he was choking back tears. He swore to me not to tell anyone, but I had to tell my husband. I couldn't let that go unsaid. Like I said before, those two have a relationship that people search for their entire lives.

Liam failed miserably with his plan. Charlie and him are weaker than Liam and I ever were. He won't stop cheating on her, I tried to talk sense into him, but talking to air is easier than convincing a Taylor when they have their mindset in stone.

The sad grieving girl from the restaurant? Britney's best friend, also the girl who is now pregnant with Erik's baby. She's still grieving, Lizzy has no idea Brittney is alive.

I nod my head with tears filling my eyes. "What happened to only doing the marriage thing once?"

"That was before I knew I'd be marrying you again."

"We need to start planning."

I rub my nose against him, resting our foreheads together.

My phone rings, taking us both out of the moment. Archie reaches behind me to grab it from the patio table. Passing it to me.

Josh's name lights up the screen and I sigh. "You destroyed our moment."

He laughs, I can hear the smile in his voice. "You should have seen Charlie's face when she found out that Spencer and I share a sister. Fucking hilarious. I put your resignation in, you're no longer a Basilisk."

I laugh nervously. "What are you talking about?"

"Your vote, she won. She also called off basically everything, so since there's no weapon smuggling we have no need for you. Go live your life little sister."

"What about you guys?" My heart is beating so loud, I don't know if I'll be able to hear him. Archie wipes a running tear from my face looking at me with big eyes.

"We can never walk away with one of us as the boss. Archie's free, now you are, go be happy."

I sob louder than I ever have before. "I love you."

I'm frozen.

Archie takes the phone from my hands hanging up for me. "Siren? What's going on?"

"Arch, I'm no longer a Basilisk. We are both free."

He doesn't ask why, or how. He wraps me up in his arms. For the first time in my existence, I get to feel what true happiness means.